TRUST ME

LUCINDA LAMONT

For my son, Jenson. Thank you for making me feel a love I've never known before xxxx

CHAPTER ONE

Christian was almost rattling with nervous excitement. He had never done anything like this before. He'd thought about it – who hadn't? *Surely everyone has thought about it?* He pondered while sipping a black Americano. He didn't need the caffeine – he was already buzzing. Not many would have the balls to go through with his plan. He thought he would feel worse about it than he did. But he didn't feel bad at all. He felt alive. He felt the most alive he had done in quite some time and the irony was that plotting Sara's death was what made him feel that way.

He couldn't sit still. If he wasn't tapping his fingertips on the small marble table, big enough for two coffee cups maybe with a side plate each but no more than that, he was looking over his shoulder for his hit man to arrive and to check for anyone watching him. No one was close enough to see but, if they were, they would see tiny beads of sweat on his forehead and upper lip.

He was afraid of getting caught, nothing else. The bitch had it coming, as far as he was concerned. He felt nothing more and nothing less. The only nerves he had were for his own reputation. She told him repeatedly he was a narcissist. An allegation he had rebuffed every time but now that he had ordered a kill, it had crossed his mind that perhaps he might be. It didn't bother him. If it meant he could kill and not have a guilty conscience about it, then he was satisfied. He told himself it was a good thing. The plan he was putting into place was inevitable, he reassured himself, and he was lucky he could do it without any feeling. She was the one who had messed his head up. He could have given her everything she wanted but she ended it. He had never been dumped in his life. He felt he had to end her and move on.

As he nursed his black coffee, it occurred to him he didn't actually know who he was looking for. All he knew was that the guy was called "X". The meeting and death plot had been much easier to arrange than he would have thought, had it been something he had been planning for a long time.

After another full-blown argument with Sara, he had left the office and gone for drinks with some of his business contacts. They drank neat whisky and smoked some cigars that one of them had brought back from his latest "business trip" with his mistress. They all had mistresses. They all seemed to think they deserved one. Their wives were well kept but, after children and years of marriage, they had gone off sex. As far as the men were concerned, the wives never wanted for anything, so why should they? The only difference was, not one of them knew Christian had one. Sara. They all thought he was the good boy of the group. They assumed he was on the spectrum somewhere due to his obsession with work and nothing else. They had tried to buy him a dance in many strip clubs and told him the girls would "do anything he wanted" but he always laughed it off and told them he was happily married.

If only they knew what I was doing now. I would be the

baddest motherfucker out of all of them but this is when keeping your mouth shut pays off. No one knows. No one will know. He smiled at this thought as he took another sip of his coffee. He had been so smart. He never knew it would come to this but he always knew that his friends could never know about Sara.

He watched the clock tick and as he looked up into the glass ceiling of the bustling café in London's Royal Exchange, he started to feel faint. He undid his top shirt button and loosened his tie. He was nervous but he was excited. *I bet all killers feel like this. Every single one of them, no matter what the circumstances, the thrill to do something so bad... the buzz of having that power.*

He told himself she deserved it and that he need not feel an ounce of guilt about it. He had showered her with gifts and taken her to luxurious hotels. He had shown her a life no one else had or could. She wasn't going to get away with ending it and being so ungrateful. She needed to learn that for every action, there is a reaction. She was going to learn the hard way. It was going to cost her her life. She would not be allowed to love again while Christian suffered.

After that last outing with his colleagues, he had stumbled his way back to the tube station. He hadn't eaten and the whisky had hit him hard. He was desperate to get home before his feet gave up on him. He was so pissed he walked right into someone;

"Whoa, buddy. Watch where you're going. You OK?'

"I'm fucked. In more ways than one. Everything's fucked."

"It can't be that bad. You look like you could do with some water. Come into my club."

"The last thing I need is a club."

"It's a boxing club and I am not giving you a choice."

The burly stranger scooped Christian up and led into the dingy, damp boxing club. The air was moist with pheromones and the lights were fuzzy. His new friend sat him in a chair and passed him a bottle of water.

"Drink. You'll be lucky to get anywhere if you don't. You're ready for the land of Nod." The man muscle mountain laughed as he put both hands against the side of his head and mimed going to sleep.

Christian gulped the bottle down in one and immediately felt slightly better. He looked around and had already forgotten where he was. His speech was slurred and his legs had no strength. He looked over one shoulder then the other and then in front of him. He didn't know what he was doing here or what the man wanted with him but he didn't have the energy to care either. He wanted to pass out.

"So what's up, my man? Business suit, slim build, not a hair out of place yet can hardly hold your own weight. You have drunk more than you normally would, I'm guessing, so who's pissed you off?"

"You don't know. You don't know them but I want them gone. They have ruined my life. I gave them everything and they took and they took. I'm broken. I'm screwed. I'm going to lose everything because I gave it all to them." He slurred and ranted like a madman.

"Shit man. There are a lot of snakes out there. Look man, how bad do you want them gone? I can help you with that, for a price."

He had Christian's attention.

"You can?"

"Sure can, my man. You pay the fee. I'll get you a call and you take it from there. I don't like to see a good man down."

"How much?"

"Five hundred for me and then the hit man will let you know his price."

"Done. I'll wire it over now."

"No fucking way, man. Nothing can ever be traced. Cash by noon tomorrow and we go from there."

It had been as easy as that. Christian had left the club in a taxi. He thought about the murder plan all the way home and after contemplating various scenarios of how it could happen and then telling himself it couldn't, he decided it was boring to think it was impossible. He was committed to the buzz. The buzz of his first kill. He assumed it would be his only kill but maybe not. Maybe he would get addicted to the feeling. The power that taking someone's life would give might be something he couldn't stop.

By the time he had arrived home that night, he had sobered up. Not that his wife would agree, had she been awake to greet her husband, but that didn't happen. That never happened any more. That's why Sara and his other girlfriends had happened.

Christian felt underappreciated. He was getting older but still had the sex drive of a twentysomething-year-old. He was developing a complex over his thinning hair and small but growing wine gut. He needed to feel desired. Susan's constant rejections had pushed him into the arms of other women. Susan never rejected his credit cards but she had given up on her side of the bargain so he told himself he deserved to get his pleasure where he could.

He'd had a number of casual flings, rarely lasting more than a few weeks and he was always the one who ended it. Until Sara.

After so many brief affairs, Christian wanted a mistress, like his friends. Not that he would ever tell them. Sara came along at the perfect time – or did he find her? It was easy. As easy as it had been to find a hitman. He had watched his friends do it for years so he knew where to go. He took himself to a bar straight from the office one night. He had seen many attractive women go in there night after night in their tight, body-sculpting suits and dresses. They ranged in age and body shapes and sizes. He wasn't as picky now as he would have been many years ago. He just wanted a release. He wanted somebody to want him. He had seen his ideal woman about 20 times but had always resisted. Then, one night, he cracked. He was sick of wanking and would settle for a hand job from someone else, let alone sex.

He perched at the bar and, after his third beer, Sara appeared. She was gorgeous and out of his league but she was exactly what he wanted to get into bed with. She was the type of woman any man like him would want to get in to bed with. Young, sexy and naïve.

She was supposed to be meeting someone but they hadn't turned up. Christian told her the same. They had several drinks together, all of which he bought. Anything she wanted. Enough to get her to relax but not so much that she could have him arrested. He let her do all the talking just so that he could agree with her on everything, make her think they were a match and roll into bed together. That's exactly what happened. It didn't even take much effort and he got everything he wanted. He took her number, got in a taxi and went home to his wife. He didn't feel any guilt. He deserved it. He worked hard and he needed to get laid. It was that simple.

He got into bed and kissed Susan on the cheek. She grunted at him. He ran his hand over her body and tried to get in between her thighs. She pushed him away. He didn't care. He was just showing her nothing was out of the normal. She didn't need to know that two hours ago he had a stranger bent over her bed while he had unprotected sex with her and finished inside her. He felt great about it. He was the man.

That's how the affair started and now, 11 months later, he was meeting a Serbian man he knew only as "X" to have her killed.

CHAPTER TWO

Sara was in the kitchen of her 1970s house. The kitchen wasn't 1970s – it was very modern, with lots of stainless steel, small tiles and low-level lighting. She stirred her Bolognese with one hand and held a glass of Australian shiraz in a Dartington glass in the other. Andy Williams was playing in the background on her wireless speaker system. She imagined the man of her dreams behind her, kissing the back of her neck. He would guide her glass to the worktop and wrap his arms around her waist. She would dance into his embrace and turn around to see his eyes. He would have such kind eyes. It would be the first thing she had noticed about him. They would dance together and he would turn off the lights. Sara's head was teeming with romantic ideas but then she remembered she was on her own. She emptied the glass into her mouth and poured some more.

She didn't need the fancy gifts or the luxurious hotels. What she wanted was someone who would dance with her in the kitchen. If she could escape from Christian she felt that she could be capable of love very soon. She couldn't wait to dance again and again at dinnertime in the kitchen, to wake up together, to snuggle on the sofa together and watch films. She couldn't wait to have affection on tap. She never had that with Christian.

Christian did everything perfectly in the beginning. But like a true narcissist, once he had hooked her in, the affection and romance dissipated and she quickly became a sex object. The dramatic change in his behaviour left her confused and desperate to fix it. She believed she was somehow to blame. He made her feel as if it was her fault.

In the beginning, he was in touch constantly. They exchanged messages all day long. He would find time to see her most days. He would stay over. They would sit up talking until two in the morning. He showered her with gifts. He told her he loved everything about her. He talked about what their future would look like. He said he couldn't wait to introduce her to his friends and how jealous they would all be. He booked hotel stay after hotel stay. Every time, he would tell her to have a spa treatment. He took her to fine dining restaurants and they would share their food. When a relative died and she sent him a text, he cleared his diary and went to be with her for the day. When she had a cold, he turned up with a thoughtful gift bag of medicine, sweets and magazines from the supermarket.

It was like no relationship she had ever experienced but suddenly, almost overnight, he changed. It was around about the time she fell in love with him. He became distant, less affectionate and less available. When she questioned him, he became nasty and would gaslight her. He would criticise her, tell her how spoilt she was and make her question herself. He was chipping away at her, knocking down her confidence. And it was working. She was a very good feed for a narcissist like him. A sumptuous meal for his manipulative appetite.

When she looked back, she realised that she had been happy for only a few months of their short relationship. The rest of the time she had spent questioning herself, always trying to please him and surrendering to his every wish. The compromise always had to come from her. It was exhausting and every time she got close to throwing the towel in, he would revert back to being the Christian she had first met. But only for a short while.

The manipulation and control had been slow but well planned-out and gradually she was going from a vibrant woman to a blank canvas. She was empty. She was sad. She began to develop a depression. Sara's friends saw her deteriorate and begged for her to end it. She knew they were right but every time she built up the courage to end it, he would revert back to phase one and brainwash her into staying. She must have tried to end it with him 10 times but every time he would tell her she was crazy and overreacting and that they were great together. She would tell him she was starved of affection and romance, he promised to deliver and a week later she would be at rock bottom again.

Last week she ended it. In her mind, it was over. She knew he would keep trying to worm his way back in for another feed of her energy like the vampire that he was but as long as she didn't have to see him, she could stand her ground.

George came into her life at the right time. She had never been short of offers but she had not been able to make the jump all the while Christian had his claws in her. She had been on dates that friends had arranged and she would have a nice time and then Christian would go back to phase one and again she would want him and only him. He was like heroin and she was fighting what seemed like a hopeless battle. She was convinced if he stayed away from her, she could move on successfully – and soon.

She met George at the doctor's surgery. She had made an appointment to ask her doctor if he could recommend a therapist who could help her break away from an abusive, controlling relationship. As she was making her way into the building, she spotted a handsome man trying to help an elderly lady out of his car. She went over and asked if she could help. The lady gratefully took their arms and she walked between the two of them into the building.

That lady went on to confide in Sara that her son George needed a woman like her in his life and that he had been single for too long. George looked tolerantly embarrassed as she told Sara she didn't want George to leave it as long as she had to have a family of his own. Sara didn't pry but she did seem rather old to have a son of George's age. *She must be in her eighties*, Sara thought.

George was attractive. He was tall with sandy coloured hair and pale blue eyes. *If a beach could look like a person, it would be him.* He looked like family, togetherness, fun and lifelong memories, if a person could look like that.

Agewise, he seemed to be in his early forties. It was his kind eyes that she noticed and the abundance of wrinkles around them when he smiled. *He must smile a lot,* she thought to herself and it was as if a knot she didn't know she had unravelled in her stomach. She wanted to know more about him. She didn't love Christian any more. The fact that she was attracted to George and was intrigued by him was confirmation of that.

Things took off with George quicker than Sara had expected. She had attempted to date men recently but was always drawn back to Christian. She was fully aware of who he was yet she was trapped in his web. They would argue, she would ask for space and in that time, she felt happy and genuinely believed she could move on but Christian would never give her space for long. A day or two, maximum. One text from him, one more wisecrack would have her smiling again and any spark she thought she had with anyone else would quickly be extinguished. She knew it was a trap. She knew she was a game to Christian but she also knew she didn't have the strength to leave. She had hoped that, with time, one more act of complete humiliation would be enough for her to end it all. She was not happy to admit it but what she needed was for someone to sweep her off her feet.

George came in to her life like the spring after winter. The world was in colour again. It had very much been black and white before now. Bleak, even. The bare trees and bitterly cold temperatures resonated with her mindset.

With George, it happened organically. The flowers began to bloom and she could feel the dormant Sara being resurrected.

After swapping numbers in the doctor's surgery that day, he did everything the right way. He didn't make too much contact, just enough. He invited her out to dinner. They arranged a time and a place and that was that. They didn't speak again until they met, four days later.

Christian had been in her bed that morning so she was on the brink of cancelling the date. Her mind was torn and conflicted because she had only ever been a one-man woman. But, after Christian had finished taking what he wanted, he slapped her arse and told her to make him a coffee. When he left, he kissed her briefly and told on her on the doorstep he would be away on business for the next 10 days. It hadn't escaped her that it was half term. She exploded and they had a furious argument. She had told him so many times that he made her feel as if she was only good for sex and that she had

had enough. He told her that he had had enough of her never being happy and she told him to leave and not come back. He said no one would ever make her happy and called her an ungrateful bitch.

It was the best thing he could have said. Once again, he had made it painfully obvious to her that he wanted only one thing from her. And so she decided she must go on the date, even if it never amounted to anything. It proved there was another life outside of Christian and his world of false promises.

She met George in a cosy, backstreet Italian restaurant. She wasn't nervous. She was too drained and lacking in self-esteem to care if this went anywhere or not. She was just glad she had actually managed to go through with a date this time, rather than cancelling, as she had done with most of her previous offers.

As she walked into the restaurant, she immediately spotted George sitting contently on his own. He was much better-looking than she had remembered as she gazed at him sitting there with an air of confidence about him. Not arrogance, but a steely, manly yet comfortable demeanour. She felt warm and the knot inside her stomach began to unravel some more.

George blushed perfectly when she walked into the restaurant and stood to greet her. He wanted to take her coat, not just because that's what he thought should happen but because something immediately made him want to look after her. The waiter took her coat and gestured to the table where George was standing. She looked him up and down. All six feet four inches of him. He was exactly the type of man she was attracted to. Tall, broad, well-dressed and with kind eyes and a smile that suggested he was nervous. A smile that said he didn't do this very often – which was a great comfort to her.

They ordered a bottle of red wine and Sara began asking

him all about himself. She was surprised to learn that George was a detective in the Hampshire Constabulary. She hadn't given much thought to what his job could be but she hadn't thought of the police. She knew he was someone with authority by the way he held his council and knowing that he was on the right side of the law reassured her further. She was in the presence of a man with integrity. As her fondness for him grew by the minute, she was also wondering what on earth had kept her with Christian for so long. They didn't share a single value in common. He was every parent's worst nightmare. *Why couldn't I see that before?*

It was George's turn to ask about her. After asking the usual, unassuming questions, Sara was caught dead in her tracks when he asked her something she hadn't prepared for.

"How long have you been single?"

The heat rose to her cheeks as she thought about the best way to answer his direct question. Her mind took her back to images of her and Christian naked in bed together earlier that day. As she quickly raced through possible answers in her head, she remembered what he did for a living and decided she had no choice.

"I am very newly single."

She raised her eyes away from her plate and met his, feeling ashamed. She took a sip of her wine and exhaled.

George placed his hand on top of hers.

"It's OK if you don't want to talk about it now but I am looking for someone who is single. If that isn't you, let's enjoy our dinner and leave it there."

Sara knew she would be mad to miss out on this. It needed to be explored further and she had 10 days of Christian being "on business" to get to know George.

"I am single. Really, I am. I'm sorry, it's just that you came along unexpectedly and I don't normally jump from one thing to the next. I am a believer in fate, though, so I am happy to be here. I'm happy we are having dinner together and although I've only had my starter, I already know I would like to see you again."

George squeezed her hand this time, smiled and blushed. She could tell she would have the ability to hurt this man and she was not prepared to do that. For the next 10 days, she was single and she would deal with Christian when she saw him – whenever that might be.

She deserved a life with someone who wanted her completely and so she had to see if she could have that with George.

The pair talked and talked and had more wine than they should have. They hadn't realised they were the last ones in the restaurant and ended up laughing as they left at how long they had been in there and how the staff must have been desperate for them to get out.

Sara got in a taxi. George had offered to accompany her but she said no. She really needed to take her time. She was sure he was a gentleman but her home was her safe place and she didn't want him having her address just yet. Policeman or no policeman. *You never know who the nutters are these days,* she thought. That way, there would be no chance of bunches of flowers arriving and surprise visits.

She didn't want anything to scare her off because this was the closest she had got to escaping Christian's web. Her own thought process shocked her and revealed the extent of Christian's abuse. Never before would she have laid out a slow, step-by-step guide in her mind to dating but she was so nervous now. Nervous about giving her heart away again. And whoever got it this time, she hoped would be the last.

She had promised him a text when she got back to let him

know she was safe and he said that was good enough. He pulled her in by the waist to kiss her on the cheek but she turned and kissed him on the mouth. He put one hand on the back of her head and she leaned in to him. It wasn't wild and passionate. It was nice. It was soft. It was gentle. It was enough. It was just perfect.

CHAPTER THREE

Christian was sitting at his desk in his private office watching a video he had secretly made of him and Sara having sex. He was torn between arousal and wanting her dead. The excitement of meeting "X" a couple of days ago had started to wear off and he had wondered occasionally if he would miss her. *It's her own fault. She is an ungrateful bitch. Who does she think she is, blocking me? No one cuts me off. She will realise her mistake soon.*

Christian had asked X how he would do it. But X refused to share that information and instead asked for Christian to confirm that death was the result he wanted. Christian said it was. He gave him £3,500 in a brown envelope. Half now and the same again when it was done. X promised to have carried out the order within three weeks. Christian wanted it done now because he feared he might change his mind but X said he needed to follow her and learn her pattern. Christian didn't question him. He was the expert, after all. The murder expert. Christian offered him more money to do it quicker but X just laughed. He took his envelope and left without saying another word. That was that. In just under three weeks, Sara would be dead. Christian was charged up.

A knock on his office door startled him and he quickly turned off his home-made porn. With one click Sara was off his screen and soon, with one Mr X, Sara would be out of his life.

———

After not hearing anything from Christian for a few days, Sara felt the best she had done in months. She felt calm and in control. Breaking away from him was like giving up alcohol, smoking or drugs, she thought. She felt strong, confident and better off without him.

Too many times had she been sucked back in, knowing the pain it would cause but unable to resist. He would come and go, literally, and she would hit rock bottom again. She had known for months that she needed to regain control and this time she felt as if she had cracked it. She decided that it was essential to block his number. She didn't love him any more. She didn't want to be with him. When she thought about the prospect of his being with his wife, after telling her he was single, her stomach would churn. They were probably all playing happy families on holiday while she was left alone and feeling worthless. Not any more.

She had escaped for the final time and she needed to seize the moment. She deleted all of their messages, all of their pictures and deleted him out of her life. Christian ceased to exist in her world any more. She felt elated and optimistic.

For their third date, George took Sara to a new Spanish restaurant. They had grown close very quickly and, for both of them, it was as if they had known each other for years. He loved her naïvety and wanted to look after her. She loved his chivalry and felt secure.

He was an alpha male, didn't mince his words but was polite and respectful with it. Of course, the police thing was appealing, too. She would ask about cases he had worked on and, although he couldn't tell her too much, she was in awe of what he did and his drive to protect the community.

After sharing several small dishes of tapas, with George's large hands making them look like bowls of food for the Borrowers, he insisted on paying the bill again. Afterwards, Sara insisted on taking him to a cocktail bar just around the corner for a nightcap. She didn't want the evening to end. As they left, they held hands for the first time and Sara felt at peace. George felt like a very lucky man and thought he had better tell her soon but words like that didn't come easily to him.

They walked down the high street in the mild October air. It wasn't freezing but a nice autumnal chill surrounded them. The shop windows were full of Hallowe'en displays which were more spooky because it was night-time and the shops were closed. Skeletons hanging and witches loitering in darkened windows in almost every one.

Sara thought about the skeleton in her closet. It seemed too good to be true, Christian leaving her alone. Sure, she had blocked him but she had half-expected him to turn up at her house unannounced or send some flowers to try to break the ice. She hadn't heard a thing. She hoped that he knew she was serious this time but something was niggling away at her. Something that told her this wasn't over yet.

"How would you feel about telling me about your recent break-up?" George placed his hand on top of hers and took a sip of his cocktail through his straw. Sara giggled at the pink umbrella brushing against his nose and George blushed.

"I assume you're not much of a cocktail man? More of a beer kind of guy?"

"I don't drink much at all because I need to be on top of my game for work. I only drink on special occasions. I've had three of those recently."

A warm wave ran through Sara's body. She might be young and naïve but she was pretty perceptive most of the time. She knew that George was interested but she knew he wasn't one for grand gestures or empty words. Hearing him say that he'd enjoyed their dates made her feel so calm. She didn't know what it was. She had always chased fireworks but was now realising that the slow burner was much more satisfying. She knew that this was only going to get better.

"You avoided my question. I don't mean to pry but I can tell that it's had a lasting effect on you. I'd like to know what happened so I can make sure I can reassure you and look after you accordingly."

Sara had been about to sip her drink but she put it down and almost had to pick her jaw up from the floor. She didn't think it was obvious in her behaviour that she was troubled but, more than that, here was a man that was actually considering how to look after her. She was gobsmacked.

"I can't believe you are actually thinking of how to handle me."

"Please don't take it in a bad way. When you say it like that, it sounds manipulative and I didn't mean it to be. I meant... if he was possessive, I'll give you space. If he was aloof, I will stay in touch. I just... I think you're a great girl. Guys like me don't meet girls like you and I'm really out of practice. My ex said I was a bad communicator so I don't want to make that mistake again. Sorry, I've said too much. This Cosmopolitan is like a truth drug."

They both laughed, made brief eye contact and simultaneously looked at the floor.

"George, I knew exactly what you meant and that's why I was shocked. Not only did I know what you meant but I believe you. You're a really good guy and I'm feeling very thankful that a guy like you met a girl like me right now. You could be everything I need."

They clasped hands over the small, high-rise table and leaned in together. He kissed her softly and she kissed him back. They stayed planted on each other with their eyes closed for what seemed like a long time. The sounds of the cocktail bar seemed to fade away and Sara forgot where she was. Her mind was empty. She realised that this was what it felt like to be home.

The pair unlatched and George stroked her jawline. She held her face close enough to allow him, not wanting to pull away. This moment was magical and she wanted it to last for ever.

She had never felt this way with Christian. He was self-serving, always took the lead and left her wanting more. Initially she had thought she craved him and that they had an insatiable chemistry. She had now figured out that he knew what he was doing and had played her. She would feel stupid if it wasn't for the fact that she just didn't care any more.

All the feelings she was experiencing with George were healthy and she knew that. George would never keep her guessing. He wouldn't be at her beck and call, either, and that's what made him... perfect.

"I have to put you down but I could touch you all night. Your skin is so soft. Not to mention your kiss." He paid that compliment for the first time with a direct eye stare and picked up his drink once again.

"George, I think you're wonderful. I really do. I'll tell you about Christian another time. We are having such a nice evening, I don't want to spoil it."

"That bad, eh?"

"Yeah."

CHAPTER FOUR

"What the fuck is taking so long? I'd call the whole thing off if I hadn't paid you more than three grand already."

X looked at Christian indifferently. He picked up his still water with lemon and sipped it. He was smart. He was dressed all in black with black cowboy boots, black jeans, a black V-neck top revealing a broad chest, and a black leather jacket. His nails were clipped short. He wore no jewellery, not even a watch. There was nothing distinctive about him apart from his stature and the fact that he wore only black. Even the all-black outfit was clever. He didn't look odd all in black. He wasn't wearing gothic dress. He was more like Antonio Banderas in Desperado but with less hair. His hair was shaved short all over with no particular style. His eyebrows were neat and he was clean-shaven.

"Another job came in. I am working on yours." His Serbian accent was the most memorable thing about him. Deep, gravelly and unnerving.

"Another fucking job? I have paid you to do my job."

Christian slammed his fist on the table and looked around to find people looking at him curiously.

"You punch table again, I leave."

"OK," Christian whispered and then lowered his head and said even more quietly, "When is the hit going to happen?"

"Leave it to me. It is going to happen."

"Yes, but when?"

"You can't just kill someone without thought and get away with it. I won't go to prison for this. Couple of weeks. Tell me again, you want her dead, yes?"

Christian paused for a minute and inhaled deeply, puffing out his chest, which was about half the width of X's.

"Yes. Kill the bitch."

———

X had begun scouting out the street that Sara lived on. It was a quiet neighbourhood made up of 1970s-style houses with gardens both at the front and the back. A lot of them had extensions or had been modernised and there was the odd one dotted about that hadn't been touched since it was built. Some owners had turned their front garden into a driveway but the majority had lawn and flowerbeds with a path leading up to the door.

Sara's had the garden and path, much to X's disappointment. Cars on the drive would have made his entrance easier to hide. Creeping around in the dead of night is much easier with a car to hide behind. An open lawn, not so much. He continued to walk to find out what the back of the house was like. As he turned the corner, he found some children playing football. As the ball rolled close to his feet, he kicked it and aimed it perfectly to land in Sara's back garden.

"Sorry, boys, I get back for you," he said in his best broken English accent.

He put one hand on top of the fence and vaulted over effortlessly in what the boys thought was an incredibly cool manoeuver. He had about 30 seconds to take in as much as he could while scooping up the ball and leaving the garden. The garden was lawn, which was a plus, but the glass patio doors were not the result he was hoping for. The kitchen window was ajar. *She could have a cat,* he thought. The frosted bathroom window upstairs was also ajar and showed no signs of recent steam, telling him she had been out for a while, presumably at work. Bedroom curtains were open. Nothing out of the ordinary that he could see. He leapt back over the fence and gave the retrieved ball back to the boys with a nod and a smile.

George was driving along Meadow Grove to leave some flowers on Sara's doorstep. For him, it was more personal than having them delivered, would be a nicer surprise for her when she got home and didn't require the instant gratification of handing them over in person. It was also perfect for a shy man like him, but that wasn't the main reason. The main reason was because he was enamoured with her and he wanted to buy her presents.

As he approached Sara's house, he drove past a tall man dressed all in black. Immediately he got an uneasy feeling as he looked askance at him. He felt as if he recognised him but couldn't think where from. The problem with being in his line of work was that he saw hundreds of faces for all the wrong reasons so seeing someone with even the tiniest hint of shadiness about them made them a suspect for him.

Shake it off, he told himself but the image of X remained in his head. By the time he stopped the car and got out with the flowers, his suspect was out of sight. The other problem with being in his job was that when he got a hunch, he was usually right. Having recently found Sara, who had brightened his life more than he could imagine, he suddenly felt very protective of her and was worried about who this misfit was that he couldn't get out of his head. *A burglar? A car thief? A scam salesperson? No, not the last one. He wouldn't have been all in black.* It was the lack of distinctive clothing that told him that he had correctly labelled the man a suspect. It makes the police's work that much harder when the witness says, "Dressed in black, short hair, no tattoos. Nothing stood out." A needle in a haystack is what their suspect looks like.

George left the flowers in the alcove by Sara's front door. White lilies and pink roses. They were bright and cheerful, just like her, he had thought when he saw them. He got back into his car and made his way back to the station, doing an extra lap just in case he saw his suspect. He didn't and, for a man on foot, he had seemingly disappeared remarkably quickly.

Back at his desk with a hot cup of tea and a chocolate biscuit, he couldn't get the man in black out of his head.

"Something bothering you, George?" asked his colleague, Mel.

"Yeah. I saw someone today. Looked odd but wasn't doing anything, I've just got a hunch. I did a little drive around the area and couldn't see him anywhere. It just seemed really odd."

"What area?"

"Meadow Grove, just off Satchell Lane."

"Who do you know round there? Hang on, is it this new squeeze you've got? Is that where she lives? Just popped out for 'lunch' did you and spotted the bogie man lurking near your princess's house?"

"I was dropping something off," said George, not rising to her bait, "and I saw this guy. Quite tall and dressed in black. He was on foot and... I don't know. I just got a hunch."

"Well, we all know about your hunches. You can smell a rat

before it's even left the sewer. You've never been wrong with any of your hunches."

"I know. That's what's bothering me."

———

X was in the basement of a rented flat that belonged to one of his circle. His circle of seriously nasty criminals. High-end criminals. Money-launderers, murderers, skilled criminals who knew the system and knew how never to leave a trace.

He took a step back from the montage of information and pictures of Sara that he had created on the wall. By now he knew what time she left for work, when she got back, her height, her physique, everything. Every morning she left her home at 0715 hours. She wouldn't return until 1800 hours, apart from this Wednesday when she worked from home. She had a car but didn't use it for work. She walked to the bus stop two roads away and got off in the town centre and then took a train across town. She carried a laptop bag and always wore flat pumps. She stayed in most evenings apart from Thursday night when she went out to a tapas bar on a date. He had pictures of them arriving and leaving. He had a picture taken through the restaurant window of the man she was with, helping her put her coat on. Whoever she was with, it was a new acquaintance. Her body language said she was being coy. This was a good thing. He needed to act soon before her new friend became comfortable in her life. Right now, she was always at home with no risk of unexpected lovers turning up. On the night of his "job", he needed to know she would be alone and he could get in and out with enough time to get a decent distance away before she was reported missing. That would probably happen at lunchtime the next day when she had failed to turn up for work and a concerned colleague, worried she wasn't answering her phone, contacted whoever they had on file as her next of kin.

Hallowe'en was just a few weeks away and X had decided that would be the perfect time. It was the one night of the year where people expected strangers on their doorstep and would answer without caution. He knew that much. All he had to do now was decide how he would complete the job. She was slight of frame and appeared unassuming so he knew she wouldn't put up much of a struggle. Asphyxiation? A single slash to the jugular? Or a frenzied attack? Christian hadn't asked for her body to be removed, he just wanted her dead. X was a literal man. You got what you paid for. He wasn't going to tell him that. He was just going to take his money and go to a hiding place to lie low for a while.

CHAPTER FIVE

George struggled to sleep that night. His hunch was silently screaming out from within him and he knew he wouldn't settle until he could piece together the puzzle. He tossed and he turned in bed before finally giving up and going downstairs to watch television.

The kitchen floor tiles were cold on his tired, bare feet as he poured himself a glass of water and grabbed a banana for some late-night mind food.

As he scrolled aimlessly through his subscription television channels, a program caught his attention. *America's most wanted*. Just seeing those words in front of him struck a chord. *Was the man in black today a wanted man?* He jumped up from his seat and grabbed his work laptop. His mind was racing as he recalled one particular unsolved case from three years ago when the body of a young man was found in a burnt-out car. The murder was for a drug debt that hadn't been paid. They were able to link the victim to a gang and, from there, they established that Miroslav Savic was the hitman hired to "collect the payment". The destroyed

Mercedes belonged to someone else who had pissed the gang off.

The police knew it was Miroslav Savic but they had never been able to find him to conclude the case. His DNA had been found on a discarded drink can near to the car. His DNA had in fact been discovered several times but Savic himself had never been found.

Although he wasn't as meticulous as he thought he was, he was good at keeping one step ahead of the police. George had often thought that he deliberately left something for them to find. In the same way that serial killers take a trophy, Savic left a trophy. He was rubbing it in the authorities' face. He had committed the worst of crimes, he was putting his name to it, but they would never find him. If George could catch him, this would be his big break.

George was wide awake now and knew deep down he was on to something. Proving it was another thing but he knew that something was suspicious about the man he saw earlier today.

He sat up for three hours that night reading through the files they had on Savic. He was the main suspect in several unsolved cases and it he his team concluded that they were dealing with a professional hitman. Not someone who just takes money for jobs, this guy knew exactly what he was doing and how to go about getting away with it. If he could catch this man he could potentially close four cases. Now he just had to figure out why he was in Sara's neighbourhood.

George did an address check for that area but nothing major came up. Someone who had driven without insurance, a report of a domestic incident but other than that there was nothing. George knew that Savic was on a job. Men like that don't just walk around quiet residential streets. And he wouldn't be living round there – that didn't match his line of work. His type would hide away in a built-up area where they could be anonymous. They wouldn't live where all the neighbours knew what day you get your shopping delivered.

———

Christian was on a sun lounger overlooking the pool of a five-star hotel in Marbella with his wife. They didn't have the kids. Her parents had taken the two boys on a camping trip for half term so that they could go away alone together.

She knew his most recent affair was over. The only time she got any attention or affection from him was when he had got bored with his latest fling.

The first affair hurt, the second was more infuriating than upsetting and now she just accepted it. She couldn't let her friends know what he was like. She wasn't prepared to split up her family and be talked about. That just wouldn't do. Susan had a reputation to protect and that reputation was worth far more than how depressed and lacking in self-esteem she felt. She and Christian had their group of middle-class friends. No one had gone through divorce. There had been affairs within the group but Susan had taken a kick out of letting everyone believe that her life was perfect.

The trouble was, those among their friends who had had an affair dealt with it openly and were now stronger than ever. Susan was so obsessed with pretending that her life was perfect that she had ostracised herself from her support network. Instead, she found herself praising her husband to the other wives when deep down she knew he was out shagging someone else. She could keep up the pretence. There was no other way, in her opinion.

She saved her tears for the privacy of her morning shower, when she bothered to have one. Her depression had gone up a notch this year and she wasn't even bathing every day. For every morning that she was home alone while Christian was "away on business", her soul suffered a new dent. She had stopped asking questions because she didn't want to hear the lies any more. It hurt less to turn a blind eye.

Christian was good with the kids. He was constantly ferrying them around to their clubs, to see their friends and being the general "pillar of the community" and she hated it but they adored him and she was not going to be the one to break up their *happy* home.

She would keep their marriage afloat at whatever cost. He could sleep with whoever he wanted. Sometimes she would go for a material uplift with his credit card but he didn't care. He let her spend whatever she wanted. That was his part of the deal. He knew she loved the lifestyle and he knew she was never going to leave him. The marriage had become toxic. Both thought they were winning when neither was.

As they both lay on their sun loungers sipping a cocktail each at just past midday, Susan was glad of the break. She wondered if she should just tell him that he could have his other women as long as they never divorced. She pondered what a perfect marriage was.

There is so much pressure to be happy, have healthy kids, a clean home, the dog, go to work and be a great couple whom everyone loves. What if being a great couple didn't mean they were loyal to each other, made time for each other and always supported each other's hobbies? What if it meant allowing them to be exactly who they were meant to be. What is loyalty anyway, she thought? *What if loyalty kills the marriage? What if loyalty ends up destroying everything you have been trying to build for the last 15 years and breaks up the children's lives?* She gave some thought to turning on her side and telling him he could sleep with whoever he wanted and she wouldn't mind but the reaction in her stomach told her otherwise.

She gazed over to look at him after noticing that they hadn't made a lot of conversation this morning and caught him looking at a group of young women, all varying in shapes, sizes and amount of clothing but all irritatingly sexy and looking for trouble. They were playing animatedly in the pool with an inflatable ball, gagging for the attention from anyone who could see them and they were winning. Either they were winning or the thong bikinis were. Susan decided to invest her time in reading her book and sipping her Mai Tai.

After getting bored with staring at the tanned bottoms and barely covered breasts bouncing around in the swimming pool, Christian was brought back to thoughts of Sara. He was getting agitated by her silence. Up until that last argument, they had been happy and they had always bounced back from arguments. She couldn't resist him and he was perturbed by how she was managing to keep away this time.

He picked up his phone and started drafting an email. He wrote out several attempts that were all deleted one after the other. He wasn't going to grovel, that wasn't his style. He knew he could have her, *she is obviously just playing a bit harder to get this time. X had said she wouldn't be dead yet so there is no good reason for her to be ignoring me for this long.*

Then it occurred to him, given that he had arranged her death, it might look odd if he wasn't in touch with her. Surely when the body is found, if it is found, the police would examine her phone, he mused. *Maybe I shouldn't send anything – don't want to look suspicious*, he thought. *Contact or no contact? What is more suspicious?* Christian was getting flustered with how to play this out.

He opted for the safety purchase. A £50 bouquet of flowers to be delivered with a note saying: "I love you. We can make this work. Trust me xxxx." That would spark her interest. *I love modern technology. Oblivious wife by my side, loving me for this trip. Secretly sending bouquets of flowers to my much younger girlfriend in another country.* He smirked.

By this point, Christian was feeling aroused. He always did in the heat and those girls playing in the pool had got him feeling horny. He wondered for a couple of minutes if he should invite Susan upstairs but he hadn't fancied her for years. He needed to be drunk to sleep with her these days. He got up from his sun lounger and placed the book he had been pretending to read face down. As he arched his back and stretched with a moan, Susan asked him where he was going.

"Toilet," he said without even looking around.

Christian let himself in to their light and airy hotel room with its sea views. He opened the balcony doors before going to the bathroom. He turned on the taps and retrieved his phone from his swimming shorts. He began to masturbate over his collection of photos of Sara. Pictures she had sent him. Pictures he had taken. His own personal porn stash. She was hot and she knew it. It didn't take him long. A quick wank gave him quick relief followed by a quick surge of rage. He was furious that she was ignoring him and she would pay the ultimate price. He threw his phone in anger across the room.

On his way back down to the pool, Christian got Susan a Kir Royale from the bar and as he bent down to give it to her, he kissed her on the neck. She smiled and felt a rush of heat between her legs. That was her problem, she had always been needy. All it took was the smallest amount of attention from her husband to feel satisfied.

CHAPTER SIX

George and Sara were just getting ready to head out to the local pub for a couple of drinks before returning to hers for takeaway night. She was dressed in a pair of skinny jeans, a V-neck sweater and trainers. Once again, she looked cool without even trying to. She wasn't wearing any make up. Her bright blonde hair fell around her shoulders and her pale green eyes sparkled. They brought out her freckles, which she hated but George thought were cute.

George wore a long-sleeved shirt tucked into jeans. He looked handsome, without trying to. They had spent the last six evenings out of seven together. When they weren't together, they were texting hourly.

"You look sensational, do you know that?" He put his arms around her waist and kissed her hard on the lips. "I still have to keep pinching myself. Happy almost two-week anniversary."

"Happy almost two-week anniversary," she beamed back at him. "I think you have actually saved my life, you know."

"How so?"

"Let's just say, you are the best choice I have made in a long time."

They began to kiss in the hallway as only a couple who have been dating for almost two weeks kiss. The pub could have easily been cancelled if it weren't for the interruption of the doorbell drawing a halt to their passionate embrace.

"Are you expecting someone?"

"No. I'm not. Who turns up without sending a text these days?" Sara looked through the peephole and could see a big bunch of flowers and her heart sank. She knew it had been too good to be true. She was dreading Christian's business trip coming to an end and now it would seem he was paving the way for his return.

Sara gingerly opened the front door feeling George's eyes taking in everything and wondering what she would tell him. The cold October air swept over her body as quickly as the dread she had felt knowing he was back. She thanked the driver and closed the door quietly.

She turned to face George but kept her eyes on the ground. She stepped towards him and put her head in his shoulder.

"I'm sorry."

He wrapped his arms around her.

"What for?"

"I thought he had gone."

"Who?"

"Let's discuss it over a large glass of wine, please."

"Of course." He lifted her jacket from one of the coat hooks on the wall and held it politely for her to shrug it on. He kissed her on the forehead, opened the front door and presented his arm to link hers into. She smiled and felt a different wave come over her. This one was warm and inviting.

———

"It was just under a year ago. I wasn't in a great place. They had just announced redundancies at my firm and, although I hadn't lost my job, I knew I would in the next round. Some good friends of mine had lost their posts. Young professionals with big mortgages and young families or trying for babies. It was sad. We used to go to this bar every Friday for after-work drinks. Normally it was to celebrate the end of the week but this time it was to say goodbye to familiarity and to welcome in uncertainty. So, as you can imagine, we drank more than normal. I was waiting for one of my friends from the accounts department but she never showed. Then I saw him, Christian, at the end of the bar, alone. I had seen him in there before and so I smiled at him and he smiled back. The evening progressed and, look, you don't want the details but, you know what happened next. I was really quite drunk. The last time I had had a one-night stand was when I was 17. I didn't expect to hear from him again. I just wanted to be bad for one night. To my amazement, I did hear back from him. In fact, it was as if he was obsessed with me. I was caught off-guard and he made me happy. It was my friends who pointed out that he must be married. I had never even thought to ask. I just bought into him and the whirlwind. We had three amazing months together. It was like a Hollywood movie, no joke. The lavish gifts and trips. It was crazy. Anyway, all was well until I confronted him about being married. He changed. He became aggressive. He tried to suggest that I'd known all along and then said I must have been thick if I hadn't realised. It was odd. I'll never forget that conversation. It was as if I saw him shapeshift into a monster. He went through an emotional rainbow going from rage, to disbelief, to deflection and then to tears. Somehow, I ended up apologising to him. Well, that was eight months ago and I have been trying to break away ever since but it's as if he won't take no for an answer."

George looked pensive. Something told him that this Christian character was bad news. He was obviously bad news but, in his experience, these men didn't give up until they got what they wanted or caused some damage.

"Sorry, I've said too much, haven't I?"

"Don't be sorry. I asked you." He placed his hand on her knee. She took a sip of her dry white wine and he took a sip of his Cabernet Sauvignon.

"Does he scare you?"

"Yes and no."

"OK, I tell you what. Let's enjoy our evening. Forget him. I'll take the flowers into the office for the girls tomorrow. Shame to waste them... and don't worry, I'll buy you some better ones. Then we can pick this conversation up over a coffee instead of alcohol. Sara, you can trust me. I just know that some jilted lovers don't always go away easily. I will keep you safe."

She leaned into her beau and they enjoyed the crackling of the open fire while holding each other for a moment.

That evening, George and Sara made love for the first time. It wasn't wild, it wasn't dirty, it was lovemaking. He was slow and sensual, attentive and focused. She felt as if she had been carried away to a desert island. She couldn't hear anything apart from his gentle breathing. She couldn't see anything apart from his eyes gazing into hers. The way they moved together was as if they had been lovers for a long time. Afterwards they lay in each other's arms and Sara knew she was falling for this man. For George, he was already there. He was in love with his naïve, yet smart, beautiful girl. He wanted to be her protector.

The next morning, George crept out of bed quietly. His body accidentally took the cover with him to reveal Sara's perfect body. She was lying on her side, her knees slightly bent and her long blonde hair cascading over the pillow she lay on. He leaned down and pecked her on the forehead and smiled at the freckles that she hated so much. She was right, they did give her a youthful look but he smiled at how sweet they were.

Once showered and dressed, he placed a mug of hot tea on Sara's bedside table. He perched himself on the thin sliver of bed available and kissed her awake. She stirred bashfully.

"What time is it?"

"It's still early. You can get another 30 minutes or so, I think. Have a great day. Last night was amazing."

He kissed her again and waved goodbye.

On the way out, he picked up the flowers that had been delivered to Sara the night before. He hoped they wouldn't lead to anything but he had some enquiries to make.

———

"Hello, Rosie's Posies. Rosie speaking..."

"Hi Rosie. You took an order for a bouquet of flowers yesterday and had them sent to a Sara Edgerton. I need some more information, in particular, who bought and paid for them?"

"I'm afraid I can't give out that information, sir. It's confidential." The woman on the end of the phone didn't sound old enough to run a florist's, he thought, but that didn't mean she wasn't older than she sounded.

"My name is Detective Inspector Ramsay. It concerns a case I am looking at. A case involving harassment. I can give you my badge number or I can come in and see you..."

"No, it's OK. Hold on a minute..."

As George waited, something told him that all was not well. He knew he didn't know anything yet but in his experience, most jilted lovers who didn't take no for an answer became dangerous. This wasn't about his love for Sara. He was married to his job. He could sniff out trouble way ahead any of his colleagues. He didn't look for it deliberately, it found him. If Sara's ex was dangerous then it needed dealing with. Even more so because he'd fallen in love with her.

"Hello?"

"Yeah..."

"It was a Mr Christian Jones."

"And the card he used to pay?"

"Um... I don't know if..." Rosie hesitated.

"Miss, with all due respect..."

Rosie gave the credit card details and George put the phone down, armed with the information he needed to get started.

Luck was on his side so far. After a quick search in the database he found Christian's details. He had been a witness to a road traffic collision three years earlier. George had his address, his date of birth, his credit-card details but there was no recorded history of any criminal behaviour. Christian's phone number was on the database. George hurriedly wrote it down on a scrap of paper and stuffed it into his pocket.

Picking up the bouquet of flowers, he placed them on Maureen's desk. If the expression "blown away" was a look on someone's face, Maureen had nailed it.

"They're not from me. They are from an unwanted admirer but I didn't want to see them go to waste."

Maureen looked less jubilant after this announcement but was nevertheless still enthralled with her gift. George was the only one that gave her the time of day in that office. He always took the time to say hello and he always said thank you for the statements she had copy-typed for him. He was the only one who noticed when she had her hair cut differently and once even complimented her earrings. He would be her dream man if he were 10 years older.

George walked unwaveringly through the office, down the stairs, in the lift to level three and in to the surveillance department. He knew Joe was in this morning and Joe was just the man who would help him without getting all jobsworth about it.

Looking around behind him and ensuring they were alone, George retrieved the piece of paper from his pocket and handed it to Joe.

"I want as much information as is possible from this number."

"Who is it?"

"I have a hunch. It's not a case yet but I can see it becoming one."

"Not a case?"

"It's Sara's ex."

"Sara. The girl that has put a spring back in your step, made you shave daily and wear aftershave at all times?"

"That's the one." George blushed but he wasn't too proud to deny it.

"I didn't have you down as the jealous type."

"Ha. No, it's not that. I have a bad feeling about this guy. He's married but won't leave her alone."

"Oh, one of those. Always ends in tears for one if not all parties involved."

"I know. I just want to see if there is any threat."

"What do you want to know?"

"Can we see his messages?"

"Depends what phone he has and if it's locked."

'OK. Well what about locations? Can you get me the data of where he has been recently?'

"That should be fairly straightforward. I'll see what I can do. I might have some info for you by this afternoon."

"Thanks, Joe." George slipped him a £20 note to ensure it was done speedily.

As he made his way back up to the office, his stomach warmed to see that Sara had sent him a text message already.

"The bed is cold without you. Come over tonight? xx"

"I would love to xx"

He smiled his way back to his desk. Maureen placed a warm white coffee in front of him and gave him a motherly grin.

"She's a lucky girl."

George thanked her for the coffee and pretended to look at his emails. He did not want to get into a conversation with Maureen about his love life, even if she did mean well.

———

Sara was getting ready for work. She was applying her make up while dancing to music on the radio. She never used to put the radio on in the morning. That was a new development since George had come along. She massaged her foundation into her skin and noticed how her eyes sparkled now, how her cheeks were flushed and how her crows' feet were more visible since George had been around, making her smile more. Her phone bleeped to tell her she had a text. She assumed it would be George replying to her invitation over to hers this evening. It was an unknown number.

"Babe. I know you're mad but you can't keep this up. I'm home tomorrow. I want to come and see you. Lunch in bed? xxxx"

Sara's heart sank. She had hoped Christian would go away quietly but deep down she knew that was not likely. He had never let her go. They had argued and she would call him everything under the sun. She would threaten to tell his wife, his kids, his colleagues but none of it bothered him. He kept coming back every time. She even told him she didn't love him but he kept coming with the presents and the trips away and false promises.

This time was different. She really liked George. He was a healthy choice. He was good for her. He was a decent man. She ignored the message and threw her phone into her handbag and turned off the radio. Work was going to be a good distraction today.

As she left her home, a tall man who stood at least six feet tall was standing at the end of her path. He was dressed all in black and she was fairly certain she had never seen him before. He was examining a map.

"Are you lost?" she asked him.

"Yes. I look for Rose Garden but can't find on map?"

"It's the road behind this one. Just go left there and left again. Rose Gardens." She smiled and went to make her way past.

"Thank you, pretty lady." His compliment sent a sudden chill down her spine and she didn't know why. Suddenly she felt very unnerved. The man hadn't moved so she made a start on her journey and could sense him walking close behind her.

Sara tried to walk at a good pace but without showing fear. She could hear her new friend in close pursuit. She didn't want to walk too quickly and let him know she was afraid. She was probably imagining it anyway, she told herself. *How many strangers actually follow people and attack them?* She thought and told herself she was being ridiculous. He was obviously new to the neighbourhood and then she wondered whether or not she was being racist. Was it because he was foreign that she was afraid? Again, she told herself she was being ridiculous and that she was right to have her wits about her and it was nothing to do with her being racist or prejudice or a xenophobe. Christian's constant put-downs and insults had her even questioning if she was racist now. Her confidence was much lower than before she had met him. But as for right now, she was just aware, really aware that this man seemed to be following her.

She made it to the bus stop in one piece and her unwanted companion stood just a few feet away from her. She took her phone out and decided to send George a text. Mainly because she couldn't stop thinking about him but also to let the stranger know that she was in contact with people and that he would be stupid to attack her now.

Sara boarded the bus alone, to her relief. It was only a short bus journey but it was long enough to have serious words with herself about how ridiculous she was and to ponder what on earth she had to be so paranoid about. She was not nearly attractive or interesting enough to be attacked at random. She was far too plain, in her opinion.

She sent George a message: "I wish I didn't have to work and you didn't have to work and we could just stay in bed all day. In each other's arms and never unlock. (I know how that wouldn't actually be possible but just humour me.) I guess you could say I like you □ xx"

The message delivered at the same time she reached her stop. She peeled on her text restricting gloves, put her phone back into her bag, secured her ear muffs and tried the ever-unladylike sitting-to-standing position on a moving bus. That wasn't too bad this time but she wasn't as successful at holding her grace once the bus pulled to a halt, thrusting her forward into a middle-aged and middle-sized businessman in front her. She apologised very quietly. So quietly in fact, that he either didn't hear her or didn't feel it was worth acknowledging.

It wasn't until Sara finally reached her desk, removed her coat and gloves and put her bag on the floor, neatly away next to her waste-paper bin that it occurred to her that the man who had asked her for directions didn't take the directions. He walked past the road he said he wanted completely and followed her to the bus stop. And then didn't board the bus.

Suddenly Sara felt a wave of unease run over her body. Sitting in her cubicle in her open-plan office with about 200 workers on the same floor, she felt alone and anxious. *Why didn't he take my directions?*

CHAPTER SEVEN

S usan pulled the duvet sheet over her to cover her modesty and exhaled.

"Wow. That was amazing."

She lay there expecting a similar response from her husband. Looking round she saw him staring at the ceiling. She rolled closer to him and put her hand on his chest and her head on his shoulder.

"We haven't had sex like that for a long time. You were wild." She smiled at him, hoping the ego boost was worthy of some recognition on his part. Christian coldly removed her hand from his chest and got out of bed.

"Are you packed? I'm having a shower. We need to leave for the airport in 30 minutes." He walked to the bathroom without even glancing at his wife. He didn't want to look at her saggy boobs or think about her hairy vagina. He wanted to know why the fuck Sara hadn't texted him back.

Once in the privacy of the steaming hot shower room he began to fantasise over his missing lover and knew he could win her back. As soon as he was back on UK soil, he would pay her a visit and remind her of what she was missing. She was playing hard to get and he liked that about her. She wasn't as needy as Susan.

Susan had gone from a high to a low very quickly. She had thought the sex was different. It was the first time they had had sex this month and Christian was insatiable. He always was hornier in foreign climates and she really felt that he couldn't resist her this time. She thought she had her man back. Wherever he had been, it didn't matter because he always came home. But the way he discarded her like a used tea bag just then was a dramatic turnaround. During the sex, he had talked the whole way through, telling her how much he wanted her and how sexy she was and how he loved the way she felt inside. As soon as it was over he crashed and said nothing and when she spoke he couldn't get out of bed quick enough. It dawned on her that he might've been imaging that she was someone else. Her heart sank. Nothing she ever did for that man would be enough.

With a heavy heart, Susan got out of bed. A few minutes ago, she'd been excited to go home with her husband after their romantic break away but now she knew she was returning to the hell that was her sham of a marriage. For a second she thought about seeking out an affair of her own when she got back but she knew she could never get it past Christian. It was all very well and good for him to live his own life but he liked to know where she was at all times.

Picking up her knickers from the floor, she slid them on and made her way into the bathroom to pack up her toiletries. She opened the door quietly so as not to startle Christian. She did not need him slipping over and breaking his neck now. As the door opened and the steam escaped like a power station funnel she could see he had his back to her and was holding himself up against the fully tiled, open shower cubicle. In the other hand, he was holding his cock and masturbating.

"Sara. Sara. Sara, you little bitch. Ahh."

Susan left the bathroom without collecting any of her things. She slipped on her sun dress and flip-flops and made her way down to the bar. Heart racing and fighting back the tears, she ordered a large gin and tonic. Her hands were shaking and a thousand thoughts were pulsating through her head. She wrote out a text.

"I'm all packed, apart from my toiletries. Can you pack them? I'm in the bar. See you when you're ready xx." She put her phone face-down and knocked back her drink.

"Same again, please." The waiter nodded sympathetically.

Christian came out of the bathroom and was relieved to see his wife had made herself scarce. Sex with her repulsed him. It always seemed like a good idea but he could never finish. She would just lie there and make no noise. Maybe it was years of being quiet so as not to wake the kids. But whatever it was, it did nothing for him. He struggled to keep an erection with her.

All he had to do was think of Sara's fantastic body, her pert little tits and he would be hard right away. That two-minute wank in the shower was more ferocious than 20 minutes in bed with his lacklustre wife. He couldn't wait to get back and patch things up with Sara. *If it went well, I could call off the kill, maybe?* He just needed to sleep with her again and see how he felt. A life of mundane sex with Susan and boring teatime chatter was not appealing to him right now. This trip away had reminded him of how she lost her personality 15 years ago when their first son arrived.

Sara was fun. Sara didn't care about whether the towels matched in the bathroom. No. Sara just cared about having her body licked all over and that's exactly what she was going to get. Hiring X might have been hasty. He could pay the bill and cancel the order. No harm done.

Christian exited the elevator and saw the root of his misery sitting at the bar with a face like a slapped arse, as per usual.

"Ready? I'll book an uber."

The morning's emails kept Sara busy until her 11am tea break. She hadn't given much thought to George. She was preoccupied with Christian's efforts and the odd man from this morning. She grabbed her phone out of her bag and made her way to the staff canteen.

Her heart sank when she saw she had 11 texts, 10 from Christian and one from George. She sighed as she reached into her bag to get her purse, being careful not to hold the queue up and start an office war. Some of the guys from IT would get very tetchy if you joined the queue and didn't have your money ready or didn't know what you were ordering. She was holding her own office mug, one that bore the logo of their stationary supplier and she glanced inside to check it was clean before using it. It had clearly held thousands of hot brews, judging by the stains, but at least it didn't have the remnants of instant soup inside as some of them quite often did.

As the coffee machine prepared her chosen blend, Sara began working her way through Christian's messages. In short, he had arrived at the airport, the business trip was a success, he was in duty free and wanted to buy her some perfume, he was boarding the plane, he was hard thinking about her and he had to see her when he got back. Her breathing became heavier as she read each message and she was almost steaming in unison with the coffee machine by the time she had read them all.

Finally, she read George's message.

"My gorgeous girl, I know I only saw you this morning but how about dinner at my house tonight? If it's a yes, bring a toothbrush and we can have some wine? Hope that's not too forward xx."

Sara felt a surge of relief. Going by Christian's messages, it was highly likely he was going to turn up without invitation to her house tonight. She could hide out at George's and that would send a pretty clear signal that she was not sitting around moping after him.

"I would love to. Let me bring the wine. Red or white? xx."

She picked up her hot mug of coffee and left the canteen. As she walked back to her desk, she was feeling very grateful that George was in her life. She would not have liked to try to escape Christian alone. Having George was a great source of comfort to her. He made her feel safe and although she felt that there was no great danger, she really felt that she needed him more than she should.

CHAPTER EIGHT

X was on his way to meet a demanding Christian. He was regretting accepting the burner phone from him. Something told him when they first met that this man was unpredictable. His instincts had told him that working with Christian could turn out to be a vexatious partnership. He had broken the cardinal rule by ignoring his gut but reminded himself that this was his last job before hiding out in Italy for a few months.

Christian stood up, looking visibly agitated as soon as he saw X enter the building. X, for his part, took in the look on Christian's face. With his eyes, X told him to sit the fuck down. Christian obeyed like a terrified schoolboy and pulled his chair out, screeching it across the tiled floor and attracting more unwanted attention. He silently mouthed "sorry" as his face flushed with colour.

Christian begun to ramble. He didn't know if he wanted to go ahead with the plan. He would pay X anyway. He needed time to think.

"Is it normal for people in my position to panic?" He was

flapping and continuing to annoy X with his conspicuous behaviour in the bustling cafe.

"Shut up."

"What?"

X leaned in and said very quietly: "Shut up. You are beginning to piss me off. You sent me seven texts yesterday. I don't want texts. Texts can be tracked. I have binned the phone. Meet me tomorrow morning with rest of money and new sim card if you still want the job done. I am leaving the country on Friday. I do it this week or not at all."

Christian gulped and protested: "That's in five days. I have five days to decide Sara's fate?"

"No. You don't listen. You have..." X glanced at his watch, "22 hours. Meet me here with the rest of the money and a decision." He pushed his chair back from the table and walked out.

Christian ran his hand through his dark floppy hair and exhaled. His heart was racing and, once again, the power he held in his hands made him feel alive.

He drank the rest of his coffee while stalking Sara on social media. Then he came to the conclusion that she could determine her own fate. He would visit her tonight and the outcome of that would help him decide which way this week would go.

———

Sara tapped on George's door three times. His house looked pleasant. It was a semi-detached Victorian property. The front door was to the left-hand side as you approached it, with a large bay window to the right and another directly above. An abundance of ivy draped itself around the front door. The front garden was small but well-kept. Sara wondered if he did his own gardening or whether someone had helped him. She could see herself helping him in the warmer months.

The light rain drizzled down as Sara waited on the step. She looked round and watched it fall under the light of the street lamp. Just as she began to worry about her hair getting frizzy, she saw a dark figure appear in the frosted glass window of the door. It opened and flooded the dark October evening with light and George appeared looking hot and bothered. He also looked rather funny in an apron that had the naked torso of a very toned and muscular body printed on it.

Sara laughed and thrust forward her contribution to the evening, a bottle of cabernet shiraz. It had cost almost £19, about £15 more than she would normally spend, but she wanted to show him she had good taste. Well, the man in the shop had good taste but she would pass off the recommendation as her own sophisticated palette. George looked a bit disappointed that the wine was what she was offering first. He had hoped for a kiss.

He placed the bottle on the wooden sideboard and closed the front door while taking Sara's jacket from her. He took her face in his hands and kissed her softly on the lips.

"Can I make a request?" he asked while holding her gaze.

"Yes. Of course."

"Can we always kiss first when we see each other?"

"Absolutely." She kissed him again and was surprised that her leg hooked up behind her. She felt as if she was in a movie.

"I'm sorry. I suppose I still feel nervous. It's only been a couple of weeks."

"I know, but for me it feels so much longer. I don't need to count the weeks. I just want to plan the future."

Sara was beginning to wonder if all of this was too good to be true. She was the happiest she had been in a long time and was afraid of jinxing it. She pulled George into her and squeezed him hard. She loved to cuddle and he was the perfect shape and build for a good hug. She had once read a report on social media that scientists had confirmed the benefits of cuddling. Well, she could believe it now.

Christian was buzzing on the drive over to Sara's. He had made a playlist of their favourite songs on the flight back and was now listening to it. Sara had sent him some that she said could be their first dance song at their wedding. He loved her for that. She had imagined him as a husband. *That can't have gone,* he thought. She wasn't taking any of his calls or texts but she would buckle when she saw him. All he had to do was kiss her hard and grab her by the backside and she would be all over him.

Christian edged up slowly to her house. He was going to park out of view to surprise her but he could already see the house was in darkness.

"What the fuck?" He pulled up directly outside and walked to the front door in disbelief. He peered through the living room window but could see no one was home.

"She knew I was back today. Now she is really pissing me off," he muttered to himself.

Christian was beginning to get irate. She was pushing him too far now. *I'll sit in the pub for an hour and come back and she'd better fucking be back by then,* he thought and sped off aggressively.

Sara leaned against the kitchen worktop and sipped her wine, obeying George's strict instructions that she was not to lift a finger. For the first time that evening there was a brief pause in their conversation and the silence revealed a buzzing coming from Sara's bag. She knew it was Christian.

She blushed, dug out her mobile and sighed.

"OK?" George looked up from the steaks he was seasoning.

He could see on the screen of her phone that she had 27 missed calls.

"Yeah. I'm OK. It's my ex. He's trying to get in contact with me."

"Twenty-seven missed calls count as more than trying to get in contact with you. It's harassment."

"He'll get bored eventually. It just makes me uneasy. Something weird happened this morning. Well, not that weird but because of Christian, I felt a bit concerned."

George washed his hands, dried them off and faced Sara.

"What's been happening? Tell me. I want to help."

Sara ran through what had happened when she left her house that morning. It was uncomfortable for George to hear. He did not want to alarm Sara or give her the impression she was in danger but George's stomach twisted in knots when he realised that the man looking for Rose Gardens had to be Miroslav Savic. Sara's freak encounter with Savic that morning, combined with an ex who was harassing her, was more than a coincidence.

"Look, I don't want to come on too strong with the protection stuff or to scare you with any police-style interrogation so let's just say that you should keep your wits about you. Do you think your ex is violent?"

"God no. Christian is a wimp. He just isn't taking no for an answer. To be honest, I have tried to get away from him in the past and I ended up going back so he probably just thinks he needs to try a bit harder. It's my fault for taking him back before."

"OK. Well, if you want me to have a word I can. He doesn't need to know I'm your... I'm your... well, whatever, but you have every right to contact the police if you are being harassed so I can have a word if you like."

"Thanks. Let's just see how the next couple of days go."

It was what the next couple of days could entail that worried George. He stood up to refill their wine glasses and check on his potatoes dauphinoise. They were ready and the tenderstem broccoli was steamed to a perfect al dente crunch but he found his appetite had left him.

After dinner, Sara and George retired to the living room with a new bottle of wine and an action film. Just as the opening credits were rolling, Sara lifted her head from George's shoulder and looked up at him. He made her feel so safe and so secure. She truly felt at peace with herself.

"George?"

"Yes, my beauty?"

"You know earlier when you said you could talk to Christian not as my... and then you didn't really say what as?"

"Yeah." George liked where this was going. He started to feel goosebumps on his arms.

"Can we say that you are my boyfriend and I am your girlfriend now? You are everything I want. I think... I think I'm falling for you."

George took hold of Sara's head with both hands and cupped her face tenderly while kissing her passionately. A wave of heat ran through Sara's body and she pulled at George's top for him to take it off. Twenty minutes later they were ready to watch the film.

George put his arm around Sara's shoulders and she leaned in to him.

He whispered: "I don't think I'm falling for you, I *know* I'm falling for you."

Sara squeezed her new boyfriend and relaxed into him.

George's mind was racing. He knew that if Savic had been hired to hurt Sara, the clock was ticking.

CHAPTER NINE

Christian was furious. *Where the fuck is she?* He called her over and over again. He knew after the third call she wasn't going to answer but now he was just doing it to annoy her. Wherever she was, whoever she was with, he wanted to ruin her evening. He'd been prepared to take her back, even after the way she had spoken to him, but he was pissed off now. This was the furthest she had pushed him. He was teetering on the edge between forgiveness and death. He slammed back the rest of his beer and left the pub.

He drove back to her place once more. He turned his headlights off and drove at five miles an hour as he got near, willing her to be at home. If she was in, he knew they could make amends within 15 minutes and have the most incredible make-up sex. If she wasn't, he was about to break into the most incredible chapter of his life. Having her killed. Either outcome turned him on.

He opened the glove box and took out the brown paper bag, opening it only slightly to show the wedge of cash inside. Looking at his phone and calling her one more time, he started to tap his foot, thinking, *Come on you little bitch, answer the phone.*

Christian drove off, knowing what he had to do. This had not been his choice. She had driven him to it. *It could have been so different,* he thought as he turned up the radio and started tapping his fingers along to the music on his steering wheel.

As he pulled up on the drive of his own home, he could see the silhouette of his wife through the window. He made sure the glove box was locked and hopped out of the car.

The kids would be upstairs playing on their consoles – they always were. Susan would be at least two gins in, due to her holiday blues. He hung his cashmere overcoat on the bannister, dropped his leather case at the foot of the stairs and loosened his tie.

Susan was sitting in the corner of the sofa with her back to him, watching television. She knew he had come in but couldn't be bothered to acknowledge him. He stood behind her and began to gently massage her shoulders.

Still not over catching him wanking in the shower that morning in their hotel, she brushed him off and made her way into their open-plan kitchen and diner.

Annoyed by another woman trying to take control of his day, he angrily followed her, grabbed her and pushed her face down against the worktop. He was rough as he tugged at her trousers while she tried to resist. He clasped his hand over her mouth and gripped her face hard, all the while trying to undo his own trousers. Susan tried again to push him off but he brought his elbow down on her cheek with force and then entered her. He was sick of his women not doing as they were told.

The next morning George raced in to work, greeted his colleagues casually and headed straight for his boss's office.

"Sir, can I have a word? It's urgent."

"Come on in, Ramsay. What's the problem?"

"I think Savic is back and I think he is about to do something serious, imminently."

The Chief Inspector stood up, ensured the office door was closed and sat back down. "Go on."

George told Detective Chief Inspector Wilson all he knew. George Ramsay was a respected detective inspector. He was one of the rising stars in his office and was on his way to another promotion. It was rumoured that he was next in line for the boss's job, not that DCI Wilson was going anywhere.

DCI Wilson licked his teeth and tapped his pen on his desk.

"All right, Ramsay. How do you want to play this? Given that you think he's on a job to hurt your girlfriend or worse?"

"I don't think we should tell Sara. She's young and a bit naïve. I don't want to frighten her, if we don't have to."

"You know the risks, though, right?"

"Of course."

"OK. Let's call a meeting in 15 minutes and brief the team. Go and get us a coffee and see if there is any news on tracing the mobile number you gave surveillance."

"Yes sir."

George got up, heart racing but feeling more focused than he had these last few weeks. This could be the making of his career but if he wasn't careful, it could be the end of something even more important and precious.

Christian was back in the café opposite the railway station. Busy enough for no one to notice two unlikely friends having a coffee. He hadn't made this decision alone, she had contributed. He was still reeling from her absence, her lack of interest. She might surrender today, tomorrow, by the end of the week. He wasn't sure any more but he had to teach her a lesson.

X slid in through the doors. It was if he glided in slow motion. Everything seemed to stand still in his presence and any mumblings of other patrons dissipated.

"You make decision, big boy?"

"Big boy?"

"Little joke. I don't have much time. What you want me to do?"

"Can we scare her? Not kill her but scare her?"

"I can do whatever you want but I need to be quick. I am leaving in a few days."

"OK, don't kill her but scare her enough so that she needs me."

X sniggered and Christian turned a crimson colour.

"What's so funny?"

"You men. You just can't cope. She won't take you back but I don't care. Price is same. I do job and we don't speak again. Where is my money."

Christian had the money in his hands under the table. He slid the package over on to X's knee.

"Now what?"

"Nothing. We don't speak. It's too dangerous. No phone. I have thrown away. This is it. I do job, then I leave."

Christian gulped at how final this plan was. No cooling-off period. But then it wasn't your normal contract.

"This is it. Last chance. I walk out that door and she gets hurt. Is that what you want?"

Christian pulled his hands out from under the table and clasped them around the back of his head and exhaled. He looked around. His head was tingling and the room was blurry. He couldn't focus. He couldn't concentrate.

"Fuck it. Do it."

"OK. Bye my man. Good luck."

X swooped out of the café like a creature of the night. The

room seemed to spin as he got up from his seat and his long trenchcoat floated behind him as if being carried by the wind.

Christian felt sick and loosened his tie. This was it. Sara was going to get hurt because of him.

His moment of darkness was interrupted by the waitress. "Can I get you anything else?"

Christian took a second to clear his throat. "Just the bill, please."

CHAPTER TEN

Sara met up with her best friend, Louise, in her local pub.
"He's just perfect. A short while ago, I thought I would never be able to escape Christian and now I am on the right path to a normal, healthy relationship."

"It's great. I didn't want to see you stuck with that loser. He's going nowhere and I don't want to hurt you but he's probably fucking someone else already. That's what men like him do."

Sara winced at the thought. "You don't think there was another one, do you? Another me?"

"Who knows. Probably not but men like him can't cope with the rejection so he will have to get his fix of self-importance somewhere. If he isn't shagging someone else, I would put money on him working on it. I bet he's never lost before. I'd love to see how he is coping. I bet he is screwing."

The two girls laughed, albeit half-heartedly on Sara's part.

Louise opened up her wedding notebook and the two of them started looking through some of the ideas she had had.

Sara was going to be Louise's maid of honour at her wedding the coming spring.

"I love to look at this book and think about how warm it will be and get away from these cold autumn nights. I was thinking, I think you should pick your own dress. I choose the colour but you pick the dress. I was thinking champagne? Maybe a silk champagne dress? What do you think?'

"Champagne is great. I would wear anything you asked me to. You know I would. It's your day and John's. If you wanted me to dress up as a pumpkin, I would."

"And that's why you are my maid of honour. My sister is trying to choose what dresses the bridesmaids wear to make her look good. I can't believe how selfish people can be when it comes to wedding planning. I never want to do this again. Mainly because I love John but also because this is a huge headache."

"Amen to that." Sara and Louise clinked glasses and sipped their wine.

"You know, if this George is as good as you think he is, and I think he is, too, by the way, maybe I will be lending you this book next year. He sounds like the settling-down type."

Sara felt butterflies in her stomach. "Do you think so?" she asked, beaming with pleasure.

"I do. It sounds as if he is crazy about you. I can't wait to meet him."

———

George and his colleagues were briefed about the new investigation. Everyone was alert but they were starting from scratch. All they knew was that Savic was on the prowl and that Sara had a possessive ex. That was it. They had no idea if it was definitely Savic. They didn't know where he was staying, what he was going to do or when he was going to do it. This was a needle-in-a-haystack operation.

George knew Savic was after Sara. It was obvious to him but he was out of his depth. He had met a girl and fallen in love with her and was now racing against the clock to keep her alive without knowing what direction the attack could come from.

Chief Inspector Wilson opened the meeting by telling the team that it would seem that Savic was back in the area and working again. Most of the department knew who he was and there was immediate interest. They were dealing with a few cases at the moment but nothing as serious as this. This type of case was what some of them dreamed of investigating.

A nervous energy filled the room as DCI Wilson began to explain what little they had to go on.

DS Watkins piped up from the back: "I don't see the point, sir. We don't know where he is, we don't know when he will appear and we can't be absolutely who his target is, really. It seems as if we are going in blind because one of us has personal motives." He caught George's eye. "With respect, sir. It just looks like a waste of resources until we've got more to go on."

George felt a small rise of anger build up in him. "So what do you suggest we do? Wait for Sara to be murdered and then hunt for clues to catch the killer? He'll be gone by then, he always is. I know he's back. I know he is after Sara."

"I admit it won't be an easy task," DCI Wilson continued, stamping on any doubts any of the team might be harbouring, "but I think we can do something. I don't think we can ignore it. We could start off with a bit of light surveillance, watch her house. You know the drill."

The room was quiet as everyone pondered the lack of facts when Joe, the technician who was given Christian's phone number, came bounding in.

"George, I think I have got something on this phone

number. Don't ask me how I know this but I have been able to access some messages that are interesting and I have also accessed some saved notes but the bit I think you will like the most is that I have been able to trace some recent locations."

DCI Wilson looked at George and cleared his throat. "Right then, guys it looks like we've got ourselves an investigation. Good work, Joe. Come into my office and show me what you've found. You too, George."

The team had been given all the old Savic files to work on but they all knew that no two of his attacks were ever the same. He was a professional hit man. He had always been able to outsmart the police but this time they did have a foot in front. A small foot maybe but never before had they hunted him before an attack. It had always been after.

Joe was able to tell DCI Wilson that there was a number that had been sent a few messages from Christian's phone that stood out from the others. There were frequent numbers that seemed to be family, friends and Sara. When Joe had looked into all the recent messages sent that he had been able to access, there was one number that came up not as often as the others but the content had caught his attention. The number was saved only as X and the messages were about meetings and nothing else. No questions asking how the other one was, no general chit-chat. Just an address and a time and the odd mention of a job from Christian but this was not mentioned in any texts he got in return.

Joe had captured the DCI's full attention and George was hanging on to every word, almost ready to leap out of his chair into action.

"This is fantastic work, Joe. I will make sure your line manager knows how helpful you've been," DCI Wilson said warmly.

"I'd rather you didn't. I haven't exactly followed standard procedures."

"OK, I will pretend I haven't heard that and say nothing to your department. I want this fucker caught. He's slipped through the net too many times and this is the closest we've ever got to him before he commits a crime. We can get him this time. I know we can. We just need to decide what to do with you, George."

"What?" George immediately sat up in his chair, aggrieved by what he knew was about to be said.

"George, this is going to be a quick, intense operation. We don't know how it is going to go and at what stage we can pull Savic in. You are personally involved and you don't need me to tell you what normally happens in that situation."

"What do you expect me to do? Sit back and wait for Sara to be murdered? Take two weeks' annual leave and stalk her to keep her safe? I can't do that. She has given us the lead. I can monitor what happens next and feed back more information to you."

"George..."

"Please. I can't sit back. It will be agonising. I am in love with her. This is my biggest case ever and not because it's Savic. Because it's Sara."

The DCI put down the pen he had been fiddling with and shook his head. "When I tell you to step back, you step back. You hear me? I can't have you involved. I'm sorry."

"I want two weeks off, then."

George left Wilson's office and sent a text to Sara, "I love you xx," and immediately received one back... "I love you too. It feels so good to be able to say that xxxx." He smiled but felt a heavy weight upon his shoulders. He had faith in his colleagues but Savic was slippery. He had to be part of the investigation. If it went wrong, he would never forgive himself.

CHAPTER ELEVEN

S avic was looking at the montage he had created over the last two weeks of Sara's life. He was hiding in an unassuming basement flat that had a window shelf of flowers outside the kitchen. From the outside, no one would ever suspect what gruesome plan was taking shape on the inside.

Gone were the days of booking into a hotel with a false name. The police were wise to that and the world was now an interactive map. They could locate you anywhere if you checked in. A hit man doesn't use free wifi in a café. A hitman doesn't even keep the same number for more than a week. He had gone through five burner phones in the time he had known Christian, mainly because his troublesome client ignored his orders about keeping contact to a minimum. A hit man lives off the grid. A hitman is part of a network of seriously advanced criminals. They have their own hideouts.

He looked around at his photos of her leaving and coming home. Mostly it was always the same time. Savic walked up to the calendar on the wall and drew a pencil circle around

October 31. What a perfect date to answer the door to someone in disguise, he thought to himself.

He put his pencil down on the desk and picked up a cushion. He gripped it with both hands, thumbs in the centre and close together. He knew how much pressure was required to make someone black out but not enough to kill them.

It would be a quick job. Next to the cushion was his Hallowe'en fancy-dress costume. He laughed at how smart he thought he was.

George was shopping for another fancy dinner to make Sara. He was wandering around the aisles aimlessly, distracted about the events that were unfolding. He caught himself holding a sweet potato for an unnatural amount of time. He put it back in its basket, loose with all of the other time-wasting potatoes and decided they might be better off going out for dinner.

Abandoning his basket on the shop floor, he walked back to his car and pulled out his phone.

"Fancy dinner out tonight? xx"

Getting into his car, he ran his fingers through his hair and sighed deeply. He rubbed his face and began tapping his fingers on his steering wheel.

"Fuck." He smacked his wheel. He knew he had to focus but he also knew everything was out of his control. He drove home and packed a swimming bag. He needed to keep busy and cardio exercise was the best way to deal with anxiety. His doctor told him so when he was struggling with a difficult case a couple of years ago. "Avoid weights," he had said. "Cardio only, until you feel better." George didn't think it was a cure but it was the distraction that worked.

He checked his phone and felt a wave of calm having seen that Sara had replied.

"Sure. I can get the bus into town and meet you once I've

got changed. xxx." George felt as if he could be sick. There was no way he could let Sara do that. It would be dark by 5pm. Savic could attack at any moment.

"Why don't I pick you up from work? I can take you back to yours and wait for you to get ready. I've finished early today. xxx." He didn't want to alarm her but he had to do all he could to protect her. The relief poured over him as her reply came in.

"Sounds great xxx and I'm giving you an extra one x."

He smiled at how sweet she was. Dinner out tonight solved one problem but it opened another. He wanted a good look in her home for weak spots. He knew surveillance would be watching the house but he needed to know where any threats lay that he could help to secure and make safe. Broken window locks, a cat flap or even just to see if Sara was the type of girl that left her patio door unlocked at night. He had to do everything he could.

———

Christian was on edge. He kept looking at his phone for a message from Savic, knowing it would never come. He couldn't stop thinking about what was going to happen. He could still keep her alive, couldn't he? Because he now felt confident that this wasn't over. They would make amends once she had had her confidence knocked. In the meantime, all he could do was keep driving by her house to look for any change in circumstances. Her curtains were closed last night and open this morning so she hadn't been killed yet.

He was exhilarated by his dance with the devil and his performance at work had improved vastly. He had secured several new contracts and knew that his nervous disposition meant he had been applying himself more. It occurred to him that he could thank Sara for that.

———

Susan was frantically searching through old bills and statements, trying to find anything. Who is Sara? She had to know. She knew Sara wasn't the first but this time she was pissed off. Seeing her husband relieve himself in that way when she had put up with so much was the last straw. She had to prove it, she had to catch him out so he couldn't deny it anymore. Christian had been clever. He left no trace anywhere but then Susan had never pried. She had always allowed him to live his business life without questions. She knew that all of those late meetings can't have always been business meetings but she had always hoped they were with the boys. At least, for the first few years of their marriage she did.

The insecurities and denial came later.

But hearing him call her name. Sara. It made goosebumps rise all over her and she gave a faint shudder at the pictures that were taking over her mind.

She had looked through all of his suitcases, dinner jackets, drawers, desperate to find something. A receipt, a cinema ticket, a love note. She found nothing. Now she was sitting in the hallway riffling through his post. She pulled out a bank statement and suddenly felt her eyes prick and the tears began to roll. So what if she found a receipt for dinner for two? So what if she found a cinema ticket? What did it prove that she didn't already know? She wiped her tears with her sleeve, ashamed at the woman she had become and decided to give up. This was not her path. She tried to stuff the bank statement back into its envelope but needed to pull it all the way out and refold it neatly. There it was. Rosie's Posies. Two payments to

Rosie's Posies in one month. This was exactly the kind of nugget she had been looking for.

Susan tidied up all the post and put everything back exactly as it had been. Christian was meticulous with his filing, now she knew why, but she didn't want him to know she had been rummaging.

Once she was satisfied that everything was back as she found it she sat down at the kitchen breakfast bar with the bank statement in one hand and the phone in the other.

Shaking and taking a deep breath, she punched in a phone number.

"Karen? Hi, it's Susan."

"Hello lovely, how are you?"

"I have a huge favour to ask."

"OK, go on."

Susan went on and explained the recent events. Karen had been doing Susan's hair for years so, although the news was of no real surprise to her, she was upset for her friend.

"I know your girl Charlie has a Saturday job at Rosie's..."

"Oh no, Susan, I couldn't."

"Please. You know I wouldn't ask if I wasn't desperate. I just want to know who they were for. Just her name. I want to look her up online and see what she looks like."

Karen sighed deeply. "I will ask."

"Thank you so much."

"I haven't promised you anything."

"I know, but I owe you one."

―――

Barnes and Watkins were on night watch outside Sara's house again.

"There he is again."

"So he is. Arrival, twenty-seven minutes past eight."

"What do you think he's hoping to see? A bludgeoned body hanging in the window?" Watkins snorted at his own attempt at humour but Barnes didn't join him.

"Departure, thirty-one minutes past eight. A slow departure. A very slow drive-by. Let's go. Now that the jilted lover has been, nothing else is going to happen tonight."

———

George was on edge and it was noticeable.

"Honey, is everything OK?" Sara felt nervous about dropping in a pet name for the first time but felt it was the next natural step. It was a sign of comfort and familiarity for her.

"Yeah, just a case at work that is a bit difficult but it will be fine. It will be over soon enough."

"How do you know that?"

George was taken aback by Sara's foresight. He had said too much and needed to get her off the subject.

"The guys that are working on it are wrapping it up. It's almost done."

"So why is it bothering you, then, if it's not your case?"

"I was previously involved but they decided a new set of eyes was needed."

"So it's personal, then?"

George started to panic and the blood in his head rushed to the surface of his face.

"I'm sorry." Sara began to panic that she had overstepped the mark. "It's really none of my business. I just want to be supportive."

George put his hands on top of hers in the middle of the table. "You are perfect. You worry a little too much but you are perfect. Another glass of fizz?"

Sara made a mental note not to enquire too much about his work. She didn't want to upset him. She hoped in time he would let her in occasionally.

A message on George's phone interrupted their moment.

Although Sara had made a mental note, she decided her resolution could start tomorrow when she noticed the concern on George's face.

"Honey?"

"It's work. They have asked me to go in tomorrow to help with this case."

"Isn't that a good thing? I thought you wanted to be included?"

"I do. You're right. Let's forget about it and enjoy dinner. Come here." He leaned over the table and pulled her in for a gentle kiss.

"I love you," Sara mouthed silently at him when they unlocked. George fought back against the lump in his throat.

Susan was rearranging her fake flowers in the extended kitchen and dusting her numerous photo frames and candles that had never been lit. With the duck-egg-blue walls and the bi-fold doors, it looked like something out of a Good Housekeeping feature. Her mobile rang. She wasn't really in the mood to talk to anyone but when she saw it was Karen she was so keen to answer she dropped the feather duster and almost dropped the phone.

"Well?"

"Hello to you, too."

"Sorry, hi, I'm just keen to hear what news you have."

"Charlie managed to get a name. Sara Edgerton."

Susan exhaled and couldn't stop the tears from coming. "So he sends her flowers," was all she could manage with her wobbly voice.

"There's more, Susan."

Susan cleared her throat and dried the tears that kept coming. "OK."

"He's been sending her flowers for months. They started off with love notes but more recently he has been trying to win her back."

"Fuck." Susan slid down against the island, defeated.

"Look, I don't know what you want to do with this but don't get Charlie into trouble. Christian is the problem. Not this Sara floozy, whoever she is."

"What's her address?"

"I don't know and even if I did, I wouldn't tell you. You already know more than you should. All you can do is control what you give to Christian. You or a divorce. Everything else is out of your hands. You also need to take time to digest this information but, Susan, don't forget, this isn't new information. You kind of knew already. I know it's still not nice to hear but you were one step ahead and the main thing is you still can be. Don't waste any more of your time with this man is my advice but only you can decide. I've got to go. Keep in touch and let me know if I can support you in any way."

Susan held the phone in her hand and stared out into the garden, watching drops of rain sliding down her glass doors, almost in time with the tears running down her cheeks.

CHAPTER TWELVE

C hief Inspector Wilson was calling a team briefing but before he spoke to everyone together, he wanted to speak to George privately. George was fidgeting uncomfortably in the seat opposite to where his boss was sitting. He didn't want to be there as much as he did want to be there

"We need to discuss a few things about the case before I can cut you out." DCI Wilson talked with a mouth half full of the sausage bap he was hungrily devouring. George tried to take his attention away from the red blob of ketchup nestled in the corner of his boss's mouth. He was a stickler for table manners. His respect for people became slightly reduced when they couldn't be bothered to finish their food before speaking. He thought it was a bit common, as his old mum might say, to see the food swilling about like clothes in a washing machine.

"I'm all ears," George said.

"I hate that expression." DCI Wilson finished stuffing his breakfast in his mouth before balling up the paper bag it came in and throwing it across his desk, aiming at the bin but missing. A quick swig of his filter coffee and he was ready to go.

"You've got flour all over your chin from the bap and uh, a blob of ketchup." George pointed at his own mouth to show where.

Wilson used the cheap serviette to give his chin a quick dusting while looking a bit perturbed.

"I've called a briefing. There have been developments. We know that Christian and Savic have been in talks. We can't confirm what has been agreed but we can guess, sorry assume, what the talks have been about. We have CCTV of them meeting in various spots in London and also more locally, in Southampton city centre. We have footage of a brown package being exchanged. Money presumably. What's more, Watkins and Barnes have recorded Christian driving by Sara's place every night. You can sit in at the briefing but please try to remain professional. We are going to decide on our plan of action, what we need from you and Sara and go from there. You will have to take leave until further notice."

George nodded unhappily and stood up from his chair. He picked up the piece of rubbish that Chief Inspector Wilson had thrown and deposited it in the bin.

"I was on leave," he muttered under his breath.

"We just didn't agree a start date," Wilson called after him.

George sat down at his desk feeling at a loss with himself. He took out his phone. Talking to Sara would make him happy. He wrote out a text: "God, I love you. What are you doing to me, woman? xx." Just the thought of her made him feel warm. He thought back to when they were lying together in bed, her small frame wrapped in his large one. He pictured her milky skin – she was so pale it added to her air of innocence. She seemed so delicate. Her piercing green eyes were so clear and bright and her long blonde wavy hair made her like a mermaid in his eyes. A vulnerable mermaid, stranded on a rock waiting for a lifeboat to take her in. She was so innocent and so kind-hearted and had no idea of the horror that had been planned maliciously by someone she once trusted. It broke his heart to think of how naïve she was.

He had dealt with domestic abuse before and no two couples were the same. Some could handle themselves better than others but with Sara, it was as if she was from a children's book. He could picture her running through a meadow, stopping to look back at him and giggle before a butterfly would land on her hand and her face would light up with joy. That's who she was to him. That was the pedestal he had put her on and he was not going to have Savic knocking her off it.

Susan managed to find a parking space right outside of Rosie's Posies and could see Karen's daughter Charlie serving a customer at the till. She went into the coffee shop next door and ordered a skinny latte. She didn't really want it but it was something to pass the time. Her mind began to tease her with ideas of what would happen next. She would get this Sara's address perhaps and could then find out where she lived, what she looked like and why her husband wanted this tart more than his wife. She was hoping she would be fatter than her and less attractive but she knew that wasn't how these things worked. Images of a young, slim blonde kept making their way into her thoughts and she tried to bat them away without much success.

She had no plan as to what she was going to do with this information but she had time on her hands and that was the problem. Time was the root of all evil. The only thing she could do to keep busy was find out who this little hussy was. She was committed now. She was too far in and now she had to know what she looked like. She had to know if it was still going on. A monster had grown within her and she no longer had control of it.

She casually left the coffee shop and put on the best, most

relaxed smile she could manage. She wasn't sure how easy it was going to be to get the information from Charlie. She had withdrawn £50 and stored it neatly in the back pocket of her jeans. That seemed like a tempting bribe to her if she was Charlie's age. Charlie was alone in the shop and Susan felt a wave of nerves mixed with excitement run over her.

"Hi Charlie."

"Hey Susan, how are you? Mum told me about what's been going on."

"Yeah, men, eh? I always knew, really." She put her takeaway coffee down on the counter and struggled for the words to say next. She didn't want to look pathetic or like a loser. She wanted Charlie to think she was cool and in control. She also wanted to plant the seed in Charlie's mind that if her or any of her friends ever fancied pulling a stunt like this, the wife would always know. Charlie broke the silence.

"Sounds like a scumbag to me. Sending flowers every two weeks for six months. I mean a one-night stand you could almost forgive but a full-blown affair? What a wanker."

Susan felt like she had been punched in the stomach. Karen hadn't told her that bit. She felt as if she could break down right there and then but her human desire for revenge took over.

"Wanker is putting it politely and, on that note, I am here to ask for your help. Don't tell your mum, please, but can you give me some more info?"

Charlie averted her eyes away from Susan's and bit her lip. Susan placed the folded money in front of her and Charlie seemed more interested.

"Look, I wouldn't ask if I wasn't desperate. I just want to know..."

"OK, OK, but this conversation never happened." Charlie swiftly pocketed the £50 and typed Sara's name into the computer. Once the record appeared, she moved the screen around to face Susan and then looked away as if that let her off the hook. Susan took a picture of the computer screen on her phone, capturing all of Sara's details and Christian's payment method and history.

Feeling guilty for putting Charlie on the spot, she picked up an autumnal bouquet and placed the flowers on the counter.

"I'll get these, too, in case your boss ever watches the CCTV." She winked at Charlie.

"Sure. You won't do anything stupid, will you?"

"No, I just want to see what she looks like."

"Fair enough. I guess I would too. Take care."

Susan smiled though she found herself feeling irritated by Charlie's pity. Was that it for her now? Were people going to pity her when they found out that Christian wanted to have sex with other women? She looked at her bouquet and smiled at them. It was a beautiful bunch and she liked having flowers in the house. Then she decided she would book a floristry course online later with Christian's credit card. That would keep her busy for a few weeks, not to mention adding to the list of online skills she had gained over the years.

CHAPTER THIRTEEN

The CID officers had been called to a briefing to hear the latest on the Savic case. Christian's phone number had provided information about locations of where he had been. Most locations were repeated but the ones that stood out not only did that, but gave crucial headway on the case.

There was an address linked to a boxing club a few weeks ago but they were unable to find the connection there. Following that, there had been a handful of addresses that had linked him to Savic. Up until the boxing-club address, his history had shown no real anomalies but since the visit to the club from which the data revealed had been late at night, that was when the random addresses appeared in his history.

The team had visited the addresses, looked at the CCTV and read and reread the messages.

A contract had definitely been made between Savic and Christian but, as expected, none of it was in writing. They knew who they were dealing with but they didn't know exactly what they were dealing with.

Chief Inspector Wilson was placing pins on maps while

offering ideas and asking for thoughts when George suddenly had a moment of inspiration.

"Hallowe'en's coming up."

The rest of the team looked puzzled.

"Think about it. We know something is going to happen soon. He is a hitman. He needs to be incognito. For his attacks to work, he can't be expected. Hallowe'en is the one night of the year people answer their door to people in fancy dress without a second thought. That is when he is going to strike. I know it."

"OK, well, first off you don't actually know anything. But it's not a bad shout. If that is the case, we have 48 hours before this kicks off."

Barnes and Watkins gave information on further repeated stalking by Christian and bizarrely, this morning, by his wife, Susan.

George began to feel unsettled. The net was closing in. "Why would his wife be stalking her, too?"

"Perhaps the affair isn't over," suggested DC Barnes.

"It's definitely over," George responded with certainty.

"The wife might think otherwise and is now conducting her own research. Maybe she is out for revenge." Mel smiled apologetically at her superior, to whom she looked up.

George put his head in his hands and exhaled. He couldn't stop thinking about how unaware Sara was of this nightmare that was unfolding behind her back.

———

Sara was shopping for new underwear. She felt that buying undies was the inevitable duty of any woman in a fresh relationship. The only problem was that she didn't enjoy it in the way she would have done before. Realising that she was only ever a sexual object to Christian had made her feel much more guarded about parading her body again. She knew it wasn't George's fault and that he didn't see her in that way but Christian's narcissistic abuse had really taken its toll on her sense of self-worth. The more she thought about it, the more she became aware of how little he valued her. Knowing that someone could actively pursue her without so much as a care in the world about how she felt left her feeling low and depressed in spite of having found new love. She held a set of lacy knickers in her hands and practised her breathing. She knew that she couldn't make the pain go away. All she could do was breathe and tell herself that time would heal all her wounds. She had to give herself time. No amount of self-help books or motivational posts on social media would give her what time would. She came to the conclusion that you can't rush healing. When you cut yourself, your skin doesn't repair right away. You get a scab and a painful reminder every time you knock it, unconsciously teaching you not to be so careless again. Every morning she put on a brave face she was a day closer to surviving that narcissist.

She had read about these things in magazines before but, as with all things in life, she had no idea the impact someone like that could have on a person until she suffered at their hands. What was even harder to swallow was that she felt the worst she had felt since it was over. She knew she was lucky to have escaped. She knew she had won against him but having finally detached, she felt as if she had left the Sara who had met him behind. She was faced with a new Sara. A more sensitive Sara. A quieter Sara. A more nervous Sara and a generally anxious Sara.

She sent George a text: "I can't wait to see you. I need one of your cuddles xx." Just thinking of this good man who had come in to her life and who wanted to protect her reminded her she was on the right track. She felt a minute bubble of confidence and picked up the matching bra and made her way to the till. The expression, *"Fake it till you feel it,"* ran through her mind and brought a smile to her face. She was in control of her happiness, not Christian.

———

Susan made herself a coffee with the barista-style machine she had bought the previous week. There was nothing wrong with the existing one but she had decided one morning, after facing another day of boredom, that she would change all the small kitchen appliances from grey to cream. Christian hadn't even noticed.

As the machine gurgled and bubbled away behind her, she scrolled through the photos she had taken of Sara's house earlier that day. It was a quaint house and she noticed how the young vixen that had lured her husband away seemed to be as OCD as she was herself. The garden was immaculate and the curtains were drawn neatly. Her mind began to wonder and she looked at the upstairs window wondering if that was the room where they had sex or maybe it was downstairs or maybe it was on the stairs. She slammed her phone down and turned to collect her piping-hot coffee. She had no idea what to do next but she knew she was unsatisfied. She wanted more. She was developing a fixation for Sara almost as bad as her husband's.

The police had put a tracker on Savic's phone number. He hadn't been anywhere suspicious either. The local convenience store, walks around his neighbourhood until the surveillance department phoned Chief Inspector Wilson to tell him he had been into a travel agent's that day. Without hesitation, Wilson grabbed his coat and made his way to the shop.

A young woman of about 18 had served Savic and said although it sounded like the man they were looking for, he had booked a flight ticket under a different name. He had bought a return ticket to Italy, departing on October 31. Wilson's heart began to race. George's inspiration had been on the money.

Another member of staff invited him into the office at the back, away from the shop floor, to view the CCTV footage they had. Wilson viewed the recording, focusing intently on the screen and never looking away for a second. He didn't even blink. A pixelated image of a man entered the shop and sat down in front of the young woman he had met a moment ago. Wilson was satisfied that the man who had bought the ticket was indeed Savic. Taking the tapes for the evidence files, he left the shop and made his way back to the station, tasting victory on the tip of his tongue.

He called an emergency meeting and the department began to hatch a plan. On the night of Hallowe'en, George was to collect Sara from work and take her back to his place. Meanwhile, armed police would surround the property in undercover vehicles. George had to get a copy of Sara's key within the next 24 hours. They would then station armed officers inside Sara's house, along with Melanie Barnes, who was a similar height and build to Sara, and wait for Savic to make his move.

This was going to make the team famous if they pulled this off. Savic had been wanted for years but every previous time he had struck, he had always left the country before they had even known he was involved. This time, they had their man, they knew when he was going to strike. He was theirs for the taking.

That evening, George picked Sara up from work and they had decided he would stay at hers. She wanted to cook for him after he had done so for her many times. If he was honest, he felt more comfortable in his own house but this worked well for him tonight because he could take her keys in the morning. He hated sneaking around behind her back and he knew it was a gamble, given what she had been through, and all he could do would be to beg for forgiveness when it was all over. He was saving her life, that should count for something, he told himself.

As they arrived back, Sara told him to go and have a shower and get into his comfy clothes. The weather was beginning to turn chilly and she loved nothing more than to curl up on the sofa with a couple of candles lit, some good food and a bottle of red wine.

George made his way up the stairs, taking in every inch of the house, looking for something, anything, he didn't really know. He was hoping to find something that would fix it all right now, but he knew that wasn't going to happen. There was a window at the top of the stairs with a bonsai tree on the ledge. He saw a gleam of silver next to it and hoped it would be a spare front-door key. But it was the window key, obviously.

He went into her bedroom and smiled at how feminine it was. She had cushions. More cushions than necessary and normally he wouldn't like things like that but they were Sara's and he loved everything about her. Suddenly, in front of him, he saw blood all over her cream covers. Blood on the pillows that looked like a hand print that had been pulled away. A puddle of blood in the middle of the bed and blood spatter that indicated a struggle and a fight. He closed his eyes and rubbed them hard. His mind was playing tricks on him. He was relieved to see the bed was pristine when he opened them again. His brain was running various scenarios of what could play out in 36 hours' time. He had to play it cool. He must not alert Sara to the horrors that were coming her way.

George got into the shower and selected a higher temperature than normal. He needed to deep-clean the anxiety out of his body and off his skin. The hot water made him feel better and slightly more relaxed. He stepped out and picked up the towel and patted his face with it. The room was akin to a

Swedish sauna, he must have had it hotter than he realised. He leaned over the sink and pushed the top part of the small window open and was startled to see a dark figure behind the fence, looking right up at him. It wasn't Savic. It was a woman. He tried to push the window open further. He couldn't shout out at her because Sara would hear. As he stretched over the sink and tried to lean out of the window, the woman turned to run and fell. She was out of view, blocked by the six-foot-high garden fence. He kept looking and saw her scramble to her feet, holding her wrist and attempting to run off with a slight limp. *That has to be Susan,* he thought.

He scuffled out of the bathroom and back into the bedroom and found his phone. It showed 19:03pm. He must have seen the woman at 19:01. He sent a text to DCI Wilson to let him know.

CHAPTER FOURTEEN

That night, shortly after dinner, Sara went upstairs and slipped into her new, sexy underwear. She'd had just the right amount of wine to make her move. Any more, and she would be asleep. She covered herself up with a small satin dressing gown, long enough to cover her bottom and not much else, and quietly came back down the stairs.

George was sitting in her arm chair watching television and had his back to her when she entered the room. She sneaked up behind him, leaning in to his ear and whispered: "Surprise." George's startled reaction was not what the one she was expecting. He certainly seemed surprised, but not in a good way. Immediately embarrassed, she secured the robe around her again and didn't know where to look, sit or stand.

"Gorgeous, come here." George held his arms open wide and smiled sympathetically.

Sara bit her lip like a scolded child and sulkily went to sit on his knee.

"I'm sorry. I had no idea it was going to be that kind of night. You caught me by surprise." He laughed.

She buried her face into his chest then looked up and asked: "Good surprise?"

"Yes of course, good surprise. It's just a bit tough at work at the moment and my mind has been on other things. Sit here with me for a minute, you'll catch a death in this thing." He felt the satin fabric of her dressing gown between his fingers and they both laughed as he pulled her in close to him.

Christian pulled up outside Sara's and was relieved to see that she was home. Her table lamp was on in the living room and he could see the glow from her television. He began tapping his fingers on the steering wheel, in conflict over what to do. His booking with Savic was final, he had committed to it and he wasn't a wimp. If some of the people that thought he was could see him now... he smiled to himself at the thought. He just wanted to see her one last time. Maybe even hold her, smell her, taste her.

He unclipped his seatbelt and got out of his car discreetly. With his usual air of bravado, he began to make his way up the garden path when a large figure appeared in the window. Christian froze to the spot as his stomach lurched with force reminding him that he was in fact, a wimp. The figure was a man.

"What a fucking whore," he said under his breath. Quickly, he turned on his heel and just made it back in to his car when he saw her front door open. The tall, stocky man stared right at him as he pulled away furiously.

George closed the door and went to the living room where Sara was curled up in her armchair, biting her nails.

"It was him. Scarpered as quick as his spindly little legs could carry him."

"For pity's sake. Well, maybe now he has seen you he will think twice about doing that again."

"Hope so. The guy seems a bit unpredictable to me. Maybe

you could come and stay at mine for the next couple of nights until he gets the hint?'

"Maybe. Let me sleep on it." Sara was surprised that George didn't seem to be too bothered about her ex appearing out of the blue. Secretly, she was a bit disappointed. "I'm going to make a chamomile tea. Do you want one?"

"No thanks, lovely." George felt a bit deflated that Sara had to sleep on it.

Christian pulled up outside his house. He was shaking and his head was throbbing. He got out of his car and slammed the door.

He was greeted by a jubilant Susan who started waving her hand in his face to show off what was seemingly, a new bracelet.

"Stop spending all my fucking money you, lazy bitch." He pushed his way past her, seething with rage, and made his way up the stairs.

Neither George nor Sara slept particularly well that night. They were both convincing themselves that the other wasn't as interested as they were and feeling the fear of rejection. Then Sara's mind drifted to Christian. *What did he want? Why did he just turn up like that? Does he think I'm crying into my pillow every night? Was he going to ask me back? In his dreams! I would never risk what I have found now, not even if I was still a little bit tempted. No! Sara, no! He's toxic.*

Sara tossed and turned, too agitated to get to sleep. George was also restless. She wasn't touching him in the way she normally would. He rolled over and put his arm across her. She rolled against him. He felt reassured and was able to relax enough to get to sleep. Sara was still staring at the ceiling.

DCI Wilson and George met in the office before the rest of the team arrived. Wilson peeled the lid off the takeaway coffee that George had bought for him without saying thanks.

"The woman then? The wife?"

"Had to be but there's more. Not long after she scarpered, he turned up." George had Wilson's attention now.

"Eh?"

"Brazen as you like. He must think she is alone or did think she would be alone."

"So what happened?"

"We were in the living room and Sara saw his car pull up out the front. I guess by that time of the evening we, she, has normally closed the blinds. Lucky really. Anyway, she spotted him right away and told me it was him. I made my way to the door and he was on the garden path. As soon as we made eye contact, he ran away like a little boy."

"What do you think he wanted?"

"I don't know. Maybe to see her one last time?"

"Seems odd to me. Pays to have her killed but is still showing up. He's unpredictable. We need to track him over the next 24 hours." DCI Wilson was deep in thought.

"Shouldn't be hard," George mused.

"And Sara? How did she take it?"

'She doesn't know.'

"What the hell, George? She needs to know. The clock is ticking and, if we are right she could be dead by tomorrow, if not before."

George sat in one of the chairs and put his head in hands. "I know, I know. I fucking know. I just... I was going to. I left it too late and now I feel like I am going to lose her when I tell her and she realises I've known all this time."

"George, you are off the case, as I said before. It's now up to me so I'll visit her at her work today. I will get a taxi to pick her up from a back entrance and the taxi will take her back to yours. We will get Melanie dressed up in similar clothing and a wig and planted in the house. This could go down tonight. If she dumps you, at least you saved her life."

"I know." George drank down his coffee and threw the cardboard cup into the waste bin perfectly.

Savic looked out of the tiny basement window on to the street above. He was excited about his day ahead. Most of the time he just had to collect a debt or scare someone. Occasionally he had to rough someone up and rarely he had to finish someone off.

His money was on the kitchen counter, neatly counted and stacked in individual piles of one thousand pounds. He had some saved from some other jobs and next to his savings were his travel brochures. He would dump them in a random high-street bin later today. His task for the next hour was to tidy up his minimal belongings and make sure there wasn't a single trace of him left in this flat.

He walked over to the wall-mounted mirror and observed his face. His eyebrows were neatly groomed – you couldn't even say they were distinctly bushy. He'd even thought of that.

He picked up his holdall and observed its contents. Cable ties, heavy-duty gaffer tape, a box of disposable gloves, a bottle of sulphuric acid, rope, a kitchen knife and matches. It wasn't the perfect kit but he would make it work. He had to leave quickly and Christian said nothing about removing the body.

CHAPTER FIFTEEN

"Sara, can I borrow you for a minute?"

Sara locked her computer screen and stood up to leave her desk.

"Bring your bag with you."

Sara looked confused and then began to panic. *Am I about to be sacked? What have I done wrong? Maybe it was that customer's order I mucked up last week.* She started to panic and walked quietly behind her boss, embarrassed that all of her colleagues were getting to see her walk of shame.

Her boss guided her into a meeting room with the blinds closed and she felt the floor almost disappear beneath her when she saw what were clearly two police officers sitting there, waiting for her. She gulped and turned to her boss who said: "I'll leave you to it. Speak soon, Sara." He closed the door quietly and was gone.

Sara shakily pulled out a seat and sat down slowly to face her visitors.

"Sara, I am Chief Inspector Wilson and this is my

colleague, DC Melanie Barnes. What we are about to tell you will come as a shock but please trust us, you are in good hands."

"OK, so no one has died?"

Wilson and Barnes exchanged glances before DCI Wilson replied: "No. But, we do think you are in serious danger."

Sara's head began to feel foggy. She was wondering if she was about to wake up any minute now from an unnerving dream. That's what she was hoping for.

"Sara, we believe that your ex-partner, Christian Jones, has hired a professional hitman to harm you."

Sara felt all the saliva in her mouth evaporate and her stomach clench. "What?"

"We have been carrying out an undercover investigation. We believe he has hired a hitman known to us as Miroslav Savic. Savic is a very dangerous man. He has been spotted near your home on several occasions. We have CCTV of the two men meeting and we have text messages arranging their meet-ups. Furthermore, we suspect that Savic is planning his attack today or tonight. Are you following me?"

Sara nodded but could not find the words to say. She was hearing what was being said but she couldn't take it in. She squinted her eyes, thinking it would help the words ring true but she was in complete disbelief.

"We've got a police vehicle disguised as a taxi to collect you from the rear of this building. The driver will take you to George's house. My colleague here, DC Barnes, is going to dress up as you and wait in your house for Savic to appear. We will have surveillance and armed officers surrounding the property, waiting for him to make his move. I appreciate this must come as quite a shock to you but it will all be over soon."

"Wait, how do you know for sure it will be today? How can I be sure it will be safe to go home tomorrow?"

"We know that Savic has bought a flight out of the UK for

late tonight. We aim to catch him in the act and definitely before he gets anywhere near an airport."

"And if you don't?"

"Trust us. He has previous. We know it will be today. It's not a case of if, it's a case of when. We just need to remove you from the equation. We suggest you hide out at George's and wait for further updates."

"How are you going to look like me, DC Barnes?" Sara couldn't understand why she asked that – it just came out. A nervous reaction to the extreme situation.

"I have a blonde wig and clothing similar to yours that I am going to change into. The DCI has George's car and he's going to drop me to your house in case Savic is watching so he will think it's you."

"So George knew all about this?"

Wilson and Barnes exchanged glances again. "That is something you should discuss with George when you see him. I told him, as his boss, that he cannot be on the case. He is waiting for you now. Your safety is of paramount importance. That's what you need to remember here."

Sara was in daze. She felt as if she were drunk or on a sugar crash. She walked down the stairs and out of the back of the building with Barnes guiding her, holding her by the elbow. She handed over her house keys to them and, once given the nod, left the building and climbed into the fake taxi waiting there. As she sat on the back seat rubbing her temples, she realised she hadn't said goodbye to either DCI Wilson or DC Barnes and didn't know nearly enough about what was going on.

As her driver took her to George's house, the outside world smeared past the windows like a watercolour painting. She could barely focus her eyes amid the turmoil of thoughts that was in her head. She couldn't concentrate on a single one of those thoughts before another one entered and another and another. Her palms were sweaty and she couldn't stop rubbing her temples, even though she didn't have a headache.

Before she knew it her driver had pulled up outside of George's house. He spoke into a radio introducing himself with letters and numbers. She hadn't paid attention earlier but realised she was of course in the presence of an undercover policeman. She wanted to shake her head and make none of this true. How could she, Sara, a regular girl with a regular job, be in the back of an undercover police car because there was a hit man out to get her?

The driver told her it was time to get out but that she should do so calmly and not attract any attention to herself. She nodded, still in a daze. As she looked out of her rear passenger window, she saw George standing there with the door open. His face was ashen. She knew he was worried and then she remembered that he had known about this all along.

She picked up her handbag and climbed out of the car muttering her thanks.

She didn't want to look at George. She couldn't look at George. The path was easier to look at. One foot in front of the other. She noticed the weeds growing up from the neat red and black tiled paving. She could help him with that, she thought. Then again, she was abruptly reminded of why she was here and thought it would be the last time she was.

George took a step back and opened the door wider for her to come in. She squeezed past him, holding herself in as if there wasn't any room when there was plenty. George's heart sank. He wanted to embrace her but he knew now she was not happy with him and wondered if she ever would be again.

Sara loitered in the living room.

"Darling, sit down." He moved towards her.

"Don't touch me and don't call me darling." She turned her back on him.

George's eyes filled with tears and he made his way into the kitchen. He picked up some biscuits, reached for a tumbler and filled it with filtered water. He took his phone out of his pocket to look for something, he didn't know what. Now his nerves were getting to him.

The house was silent and he hated it. it was more silent than it was before she had arrived. He had lost her and he knew it. The one good thing to happen to him in a long time and he had blown it.

He placed the tumbler of water near her along with a plate of biscuits. She looked at it and frowned.

"Water? Is that it? I've got a hit man after me and you give me water?"

"Sorry, I can get you something stronger, I just didn't think that would be a good idea."

"Of course. You know all about good ideas."

"Sara, I'm sorry. I should have told you. I just…"

"You just didn't because you just thought you'd like to shag me instead. I thought you were different but, oh look, you're not. I should've known I'm not capable of making a sensible decision."

George walked away and went into the kitchen and leaned against the countertop. He didn't know how or where to start. Her had never been good at communicating with an upset female, not outside of his line of work, anyway. His last partner had told him so enough times. She told him how stupid he was on so many occasions, how he didn't understand what women wanted and every time he opened his mouth he made it worse. He didn't want to make it worse with Sara – he wanted to make it better. He wanted her to know he was going to protect her. Staying in the kitchen wasn't going to do anything. He told himself to put his work head on and treat her like the victim she was. Remove the personal feelings from the situation and just be there for her and see if he could get her to talk to him. If he could get her to talk then he could respond to what she was saying rather than offering something to say without invitation and getting it wrong.

He sat down on another chair.

"How are you feeling? Can I get you anything?"

"I said I don't want water."

"I don't really think anything stronger is a good idea, it's three o'clock."

"I don't really give a shit what you think, George, if that's even your name. Once the job is done, I'll be out of your hair and you can get back to your job."

"I don't want that, Sara. Please, I was trying to protect you."

"By not informing me that a killer was after me? Oh yeah. Well done. I'd give you a medal now but I don't carry a spare."

"I'll get you a drink." He could work with this. She was angry and that was natural. At least she was talking.

He went in to the kitchen and poured a single shot of gin with a long serving of tonic, hoping that would satisfy her thirst. He understood completely why she wanted the drink but he wanted her alert until this day was over.

Tentatively, he passed her the drink and sat back down again and said nothing. She took a sip and then another larger one before putting it down.

"I feel so stupid. That's what hurts."

George leapt off his seat and kneeled at her feet. "You're not stupid. God no. Don't think that."

"You thought I was stupid," she said sulkily, looking down at the floor.

"I didn't. I don't. I've never thought that."

"Then why, George. Why? Why didn't you tell me straight away?"

"I don't know. I am the stupid one. I know I should have told you."

———

Christian was at his desk, staring into space. The adrenaline was running through his veins at such a pace that he didn't know what he felt. He wasn't convinced that he wouldn't miss Sara but he also knew that he wanted to go through with the kill. He thought it would give him a new edge. He wanted the power. He wanted the confidence that came with not caring. He was pretty certain he would enjoy the buzz but for now he just had to play the waiting game. He hoped he wouldn't miss her too much but he hoped for a news flash more.

He opened a new internet window and typed in *Evening Gazette*. He hit the search button and bit his lip. The links loaded and he clicked on the top one from the search engine to take him to the home page. It loaded quickly and the front page had a story about a warehouse fire. He gently smacked his desk with a quiet fist and then ran his hands through his hair. *Maybe she hasn't been found yet. Maybe she is lying in a pool of blood somewhere.*

It occurred to Christian that he didn't actually know where the killing was going to take place. It was never agreed it would happen at her house. He decided he would do another drive-by on the way home and look for signs of life.

———

Susan was at home, sitting on her faux sheepskin rug in her vanilla bedroom. All of her furniture was made of mirrored glass. The king-size bed was designed to look like a large sleigh but was painted silver. She had a small chandelier hanging from the centre of the ceiling. Above the bed was a large blown-up picture of her kissing Christian on their wedding day 15 years ago. In her hands were print-outs of emails he had sent Sara. Tears were rolling down her face, one after the other, black mascara tracks revealing where each tiny drop went.

She had found the details of a mobile IT consultant who had come to fix her broken computer. After a completely made-up story that wasn't lost on him, he helped the damsel in distress hack her husband's email account in return for an extra £100. The young man felt as if he was doing a good deed and he needed the extra money for a new sound system for his already modified car. He fantasised about the distressed housewife coming on to him while he was there. He was 19 and always up for it and was just waiting for the day a scorned wife let him play out his fantasy. Today was not his day. Turns out she really did only want the computer looking at. He took the £100 and left.

Once he had left, Susan sat down and saw the whole sordid history in front of her eyes. This hadn't been a fling. This was an obsession. It didn't seem like love, either, but that made the pain worse for her. He couldn't get enough of this woman and he wanted her in a way she had never felt wanted. If he had fallen in love with her she could almost understand the infidelity but this was worse than that. She saw his tone change as she went through his emails. Some had been nasty. He had a temper, she knew that, but suddenly she felt uneasy. She began to suspect that he might harm this girl if he didn't get his way. For the first time, she began to feel as if she didn't know who she was living with.

———

Melanie Barnes had changed into her undercover clothes and was wearing a blonde wig to make her look like Sara. It was good enough for her to walk into Sara's house, at least.

George's phone rang and he left Sara in his living room to go into the kitchen and take the call. Sara didn't move or even look at him. He felt low but there was a job to do.

Quietly, he walked back into the living room while still looking at his phone. He put it back in his pocket and exhaled. Then he knelt down to Sara's level and placed his hands on her knees. She didn't move them.

"DCI Wilson, who you met earlier today, is on his way here with DC Barnes, Mel. I am going to drive Mel from here in my car and Wilson is going to sit here with you. I will drop Mel at your house and she'll go into the property, which is going to be surrounded with an undercover presence. The rest... we will just have to wait and see."

Sara started to cry.

"I know this must seem like a nightmare to you but we know Savic is going to act today. I think he is going to go to your home in a Hallowe'en costume. We are going to get him, Sara. This is almost over. We will protect you. If it's the last thing I ever do for you, I will protect you."

Sara began to sob and George tried to hold her. She didn't push him away but she didn't open up to him, either. She struggled to breathe through her tears as the enormity of the situation began to unfold around her. George had only been doing his job but now the relationship was over. A man was out there determined to kill her, ordered by Christian, who also didn't love her. Christian was going to be arrested. She was going to be left alone.

The emotional moment was interrupted by a knock at the door. George got to his feet, leaving Sara alone on the chair while he went to answer the door.

"Hi sir, come on in. Barnes, ready for action?" George closed the door behind them and they talked in low voices about what was going to happen next.

"How is she?"

"Not great, sir. Hates me I think. Let's just get this done. I just hope we catch him and haven't missed anything." The three of them looked at each other in silent agreement.

George led them back into the living room. Sara was not in her seat. Her glass was on the floor, knocked over and the remains of her drink was soaking into the carpet.

CHAPTER SIXTEEN

Panicking, George burst through the door leading to the kitchen. Sara was not in there either but the back door was ajar. George hastily made his way through his small galley kitchen, knocking a bread board with a buttered knife off the surface and on to the floor. Sara was standing on the back step.

"What are you doing?" he asked standing behind her. "You need to come in. You are at risk and this is about to go down at any moment. Come inside."

Sara squeezed past him back into the house, keeping her eyes to the floor.

Chief Inspector Wilson ran over what they were all to do. Sara was to wait at George's with him. George was to drive DC Barnes to Sara's house and follow her into the house and then immediately leave.

For the first time that day, George was calm. This was the bit where he knew what to do and how to be. His nerves were completely at ease and he was looking forward to marching on with the plan, all the while hoping that Sara would be with him by the end of it. He knew he could come good for her, he could be her hero but would she ever let him back in? He tried not to think about it, instead bringing his focus back to the task in hand.

———

Christian had an urge to see Sara. He couldn't explain the feeling he was experiencing. It wasn't sadness or grief or even love, it was just a longing to see her. He wondered if, on some spiritual level, he was picking up a connection from a deceased Sara and that was why he was feeling so odd. He couldn't wait to find out so he shut down his computer, closed the blinds in his office and left early, smiling and waving at his staff as he did so.

He buckled himself into his car and the radio came on. It was playing a song that reminded him of when they were together. It wasn't his normal type of song but it had been in the charts when they started dating and it had always reminded him of them, not her, ever since. He took the fact that this song was on the radio again, right now, as a sign that he was doing the right thing. Something was building up inside of him. It wasn't anxiety either. He just couldn't put his finger on it, he just needed to see her.

When he pulled up in Rose Gardens, just around the corner from Sara's, he noticed something colourful hanging out of a wheelie bin. He looked around and couldn't see anyone so he leapt out of his car and went and retrieved the item as quickly as he could and got back in his car before anyone saw him. To his amazement, it was a Hallowe'en costume. It was brand-new, with the labels on, and seemed to have been dumped. A thought crossed his mind and he smiled to himself. Another sign, he thought. Everything was falling into place. He got back into his car and waited. Sara wouldn't be home for another 20 minutes so he decided to do some work emails on his phone to pass the time.

Susan asked the taxi driver to pull up outside Sara's house. She didn't want to take her own car in case Christian was spying. The key she had found stashed in his bedside table had to be for Sara's. She must have given it to him, she concluded. There was a good chance she had had the locks changed, if she had any sense, but Susan suspected she didn't have much of that. If she could just talk to her and let her know she was in danger, she would feel better. She had thought about phoning but knew Sara would probably hang up. She considered visiting her at work but realised that might frighten her off. A visit to her home was the only way. She could tell her the concerns she had face to face and she could also look into the eyes of the woman her husband was obsessing over.

Hurriedly, she made her way to the door and put the key in the lock. It opened. Susan felt her knees go weak. She put on the hallway light and sat on the bottom step of the stairs facing the front door. Suddenly she came down to earth with a crash and wondered what the hell she was doing. *I could be arrested. Sara could attack me. I have to get out but not without a quick look around first.* Panicking, Susan made her way up the stairs, her heart almost in her mouth.

Christian saw a faint light coming from the frosted bathroom window upstairs in Sara's house. "She's home. It's time." He pulled the zombie mask over his face and secured the black cape around his neck. He drove a bit closer to her house but still out of view. He wanted to get in and out. He needed a quick getaway. He got out of the car and speedily walked to the front door. As he approached it the hallway light went off. His heart was racing. His palms became sweaty and saliva flooded his mouth. He stood quietly on the front step and watched as the front door opened, seemingly in slow motion. Without hesitation, he pulled the screwdriver he had taken from his glove box out of his pocket and plunged it into her neck. The blood was immediate and fast, it was almost spurting out. Quite the Hallowe'en scene, he thought. He was still standing there as she slumped to the floor, when suddenly a bright light shone behind him and a megaphone-amplified voice ordered him to drop his weapon and turn around with his hands on his head. "Shit," was all Christian could say.

George drove along Rose Gardens and was troubled to see Christian's car parked up. He drove past slowly and saw that no one was in it. As he turned the corner on to Sara's street everything slowed down. His vision went blurry and his hearing went. The police presence was huge and Christian was leaning over the bonnet of a car with his hands cuffed behind his back. Police tape was being secured around Sara's house and there were police officers guarding the front door, which was open, and it looked as if someone was slumped on the floor. He could see some hair.

"Fuck." His heart was racing, his head was pounding. He struggled to concentrate and it dawned on him that Savic was not part of this picture. He quickly reversed back around the corner.

"What are you going to do, George?" Mel Barnes was worried but knew she had to keep George calm.

"I can't radio the DCI. What if Savic is there? I just need to get back to mine and find Sara."

George broke the speed limit all the way back to his house and pulled some risky manoeuvres. He could have done with some blue lights. He was battling images of a murdered Sara as much as he was battling with the traffic. Part of him wanted to cry. He felt sick. He didn't know what had happened back there but he guessed it wasn't planned, unless Savic was even smarter than he had given him credit for.

He slowed down as he pulled into his road and saw a tall man matching Savic's description on foot in the distance.

"That's him. That's fucking him," he snarled, pulling over and stopping the car.

"George, be careful." Melanie Barnes knew exactly what was coming next. George left the car without a word and began to run after the suspect. DC Barnes unclipped her seatbelt and knew she had to go and see what had happened inside the house. She swallowed and prepared herself for the worst.

George began to run faster than he had ever run before. He didn't even know he sprint like that. He was almost tripping over himself and wasn't even sure each foot was landing on the ground before he lifted the next one. He was so focused that his body felt weightless and he knew that his life was worth nothing if he let this man escape. Savic turned around and saw George coming for him and also began to run. He dodged behind a house and was heading for the garden. George was gaining on him. He didn't know what he was going to do, he was catching up with him, he was going to catch him. Savic was just feet away from him now. Unbelievably, Savic tripped and began to tumble just a stone's throw front of him. George got to him, he threw the hardest punch at him as he could. Savic took it but didn't flinch. He hit back but George managed to dodge the fist. George threw another punch that Savic caught and used to pull George to the ground. The pair began to wrestle. George knew he had to do everything in his power to keep this man with him and not get knocked out. He got a clear view of him and pulled his head back before bringing it back down as hard as he could on Savic's nose. Savic released his grip and George began to rain down punches on him. Blood was appearing fast and splattering everywhere but George couldn't stop. If this man got away it would be the end of him. He had no cuffs so he just had to knock him out. He grabbed Savic's head and smashed it repeatedly against the ground. At last, he realised that Savic was no longer fighting back. He had knocked him out. He had him. He had one of the most wanted men and he took him down himself. Looking around and getting his bearings, he began to shout for help over and over again.

Back-up arrived within seconds. Mel Barnes had radioed before she entered George's house. They cuffed Savic and it took two very burly officers to drag him into the back of the van where they threw him in, still in a daze.

George had a split eyebrow and a burst lip but began to run to his house. As his home came into view he saw ambulances outside and a stretcher being carried out. DC Barnes intercepted him at the bottom of his garden path.

"There's a pulse, George, but she is in danger. She's lost a lot of blood." George pushed her aside and ran to the stretcher and grabbed Sara's hand.

"Stay with me darling, stay with me," he begged. "I'm coming in the ambulance," he told the crew without letting go of her hand. She had a stab wound to the chest.

The paramedics closed the doors and set off, blue lights flashing and siren wailing. George had to stay out of the way while they worked on her to try to keep her alive. There wasn't even room to hold her hand.

As he watched helplessly, he began to challenge his faith in God. No God that loved him could be so cruel to bring him the happiness that he had experienced with Sara over the last month only to snatch it away from him in such a brutal way. He was struggling to hold back the tears of fear, desperation and frustration. While at work, he felt very much in control but here he was, having to leave the destiny of his true love to fate. He had already lost one wife – it would be too much for him to take if he lost Sara, too.

They pulled up outside the hospital and everything

suddenly speeded up as if they had been on pause and the play button had been hit. The paramedics sprang to life to get Sara out of the ambulance and into an operating theatre as quickly as possible. There were medics everywhere, escorting them in through the hospital, and then she was gone.

George found himself waiting in the family room, almost unaware of how he got there. He stood up and walked around the small room, looking at the posters and pictures on the walls but not really taking them in. He poured himself a cup of water and knocked it back. It dawned on him that his home was a crime scene and that he didn't know what had happened. He was so swept up in making sure Sara was all right that he forgot about his colleagues.

Hurriedly, he got his phone out and phoned DCI Wilson. No answer. He looked up DC Barnes's number and she answered before it had rung twice.

"Mel, I'm sorry. I just wanted to make sure Sara was OK. What happened? What do we know?"

"It's not clear. Forensics are in your place now. How is Sara?"

"She's in theatre, I just have to wait. She has a stab wound to the chest. How is it not clear? What has DCI Wilson said?" The silence that followed told George that Wilson hadn't said anything. "Mel, what's happened. Has the guv'nor come to harm?"

"George... he's dead. His throat was cut, pretty brutal."

George felt as if he had been winded. He sat down on the couch and held his phone away from him. Mel was repeating his name and asking him if he was still there. Biting on his own fist as tears began to roll, he took a deep breath and put the phone to his ear again.

"I understand, Mel. Just a shock. I need to wait here for Sara. Obviously, I know I can't go home – my place is a crime scene. But maybe you could let me know when I can get back in to collect some things."

"I will, George. I really hope Sara pulls through. You're welcome to kip at mine tonight if you like. I don't think you'll be able to get back into yours for a while. Drop me a text if you want to. Take care."

"Thanks, Mel."

George disconnected the call and gently put his phone face-down next to him. He sat forward and put his head in his hands. This was the darkest day of his whole working life.

CHAPTER SEVENTEEN

Christian was sitting in the interview room, cuffed. He felt as if he was in a bad dream. He felt absolutely no remorse over what he had done – he had actually quite enjoyed it. He enjoyed the power and he was proud of his own bravery. The only thing niggling away at him was how Susan was going to react. She was going to know how much of a bad man he was now and he didn't like the idea of that. He hated the thought of all their friends telling her she had dodged a bullet and how none of them had ever suspected he could be capable of something like that.

As far as the kids were concerned, he could kiss goodbye to having a relationship with them. He was going to be in prison for many years now. He could cope with the kid element. He wasn't a great father anyway. He was always away on business and they appreciated him even less than his wife did. She would take care of them in the house that he had provided, in the lifestyle that he had provided. He had enough savings to keep them going for a few years. He sighed as his mind tried to clean up the mess he had made. Then the police entered the room.

"When can I speak to Susan? I need to speak to her now."

The two officers looked at each other awkwardly before taking their seats and starting the tape to record the interview, each giving their names for the tape.

"Mr Jones, Christian, can you talk us through the events that led up to you going to Sara Edgerton's house this evening?"

"There were no events leading up to it. We used to date and I was upset and I think it's pretty fucking obvious that I lost control. I have lost my mind. She had been tormenting me for months. She drove me to it."

"Drove you to what?"

"To fucking stabbing her with a screwdriver."

Once again, the police officers looked at each other, frowning, and then back at Christian.

"Christian, just to clarify, you are saying that you stabbed Sara Edgerton with a screwdriver today."

Christian looked at them, confused, and wondered if they were trying to trip him up but he knew that couldn't be so as he had been caught red-handed and admitted everything. He leaned across the desk with his hands cupped and said: "Yes. You know I did. You caught me. You were there."

"Mr Jones, the woman you fatally stabbed with a screwdriver was not Sara Edgerton."

Christian sat upright immediately. "What?" The colour drained from his face. "Then who?"

"Mr Jones, the woman you stabbed this evening in the neck with a screwdriver has been identified as a Mrs Susan Jones."

Christian stared at both of them in disbelief, lost for words. He felt as if the floor had disappeared from beneath him as he continued to gaze at them in horror.

George was still in the family room, waiting for news. The dusty-pink-painted walls and the dim lamp made him feel tired. There was a selection of magazines on the table, months out of date. In the corner was a basket of children's toys. The sofa was old and worn and there was a bookcase that was a third full of various books. He looked around the room and assumed that the contents must have been from donations. He appreciated that they tried to make a room like this a calming and soothing environment. It wasn't a great room but he supposed it was better than a bright white room like an operating theatre with dazzling strip lights. This room looked lived in. He thought about how many people had waited in this room for news that either changed the way they lived their life from there on in or news that devastated them and they walked out a changed person for ever.

The basket of children's toys choked him. He couldn't imagine waiting for news of a loved one while trying to put on a brave face for a child. Then he thought about the people who might have been waiting for news of a child. He thought he felt his heart crack at that point. He pondered the meaning of life and again thought about his faith and beliefs and concluded that the meaning of life was to feel. To feel the love of another and to feel love for them. To feel the good in things you see and do. To feel the grief of loss and to know how lucky you were to miss someone that much. To feel the success of something you planned or something that fell on to your lap. To feel gratitude for the small things. He then changed his mind and told himself that the meaning of life wasn't to feel, it was to live. He hoped that Sara would pull through and that they could live together. He was startled by the door opening. He turned to see who it was and, when he saw it was a nurse he knew, he pleaded with his eyes for it to be good news.

"Hi, George. She's out of theatre. She lost a lot of blood but she is stabilised. We need to monitor her over the next 24 hours before we can confirm that she is out of the woods but I think things are looking a lot better than when she arrived. The surgeon did a great job. She's in the best hands." The nurse came closer to him and squeezed his upper arm. "Can I get you anything?"

"May I see her? Can I stay here with her?"

"Yes, I'll take you to her. She's in an induced coma at the moment. I'll ask and see if we can give you a bed to stay. Come on, let's get you a cuppa."

George let the nurse guide him out of the room and along the corridor. It always amazed him how good these people were at their jobs. The amount of care and compassion they show when they have to do it, day in, day out. They always seem to be able to offer such kindness to everyone they meet and he for one was very appreciative. His lip kept wobbling involuntarily and he didn't want anyone to see him lose it.

The nurse stopped outside a door and opened it slowly and quietly. He wasn't really sure what the point was letting him see her as Sara was out of it and then he realised the nurse did it for his benefit. He went to Sara's side. He wanted to stroke her head and kiss her but he was too scared to touch her. She was fragile. She was the only Miroslav Savic survivor that he knew of. Part of him was desperate to know what had happened but the other part in equal measure did not want to know. He couldn't imagine how frightened she must have been. He had images flashing through his mind of Savic barging his way in and throwing himself at her. She was so small compared to him. She had no chance. George had promised her she would be safe and he had let her down badly.

He sat down on the chair next to the bed and held her hand, being careful not to dislodge her cannula. She looked so peaceful and surprisingly well. He leaned in to her and moved her hair behind her ear and whispered: "I love you, Sara. I want you to be with me for ever. As soon as we can get you out of here, we are going to move on with our lives, together. I'm so proud of you. You are a fighter. I love you, I love you. Please don't sleep for too long."

CHAPTER EIGHTEEN

Christian was charged and remanded in custody. There was no getting out of it for him. He was caught red-handed for murder, even though he thought he was killing someone else. As soon as he realised he had lost everything, he gave the police all the information he had on Savic. He didn't give them much that they didn't already know, apart from the chance meeting at the boxing club. Some officers were immediately ordered to delve deeper into that lead and that little nugget would eventually result in a fairly sizeable organised crime group being taken down. Not only was Savic looking at a life behind bars but they had also arrested and charged four others who were on their wanted list through the information about the boxing club.

Susan's sister took on their children and moved into their family home. She refused to see Christian and she ignored his request to bring his sons to see him. She had always known he was a bad egg and had even told her sister so on the eve of her wedding to him but Susan had been besotted.

Three days had passed and George was on his way to the

ward to see Sara. One of the friendly nurses approached him, smiling.

"She's awake," she announced.

George felt a lump in his throat. For a moment, he almost didn't know what to do. He had become accustomed to coming in and talking to her while she slept. The nurse could sense his anxiety and took him by the elbow;

"Come on. She'll be pleased to see you."

The door to Sara's private room was ajar and George could see that she was sitting upright in bed, propped against pillows.

Hesitantly, he made his way in, poking his head through first and holding his body back. She looked at him, paused and looked away. His stomach sank. This was what he had been dreading. He took the rest of his body into the room and stood next to her bed.

"Hey. How are you?" Silence. "You actually look great." She turned her head further away from him. "Hey, come on." He tried to hold her hand and she pulled it away. 'OK. I get it. I'm sorry. I'm so sorry. I never ever meant for you to get hurt." Sara snorted. "Maybe you will talk to me tomorrow.' He stood up slowly, wishing for a word from her, hoping she would ask him to stay but she refused to even look at him. He walked out of the room, head hung low but not as low as his mood.

Sara listened for his footsteps to be gone then rolled on to her side and a tear slowly rolled down her cheek.

The nurse had seen what happened and quietly chased after George.

"George! Wait. Don't go yet. She's been through a lot. You both have."

"She doesn't want to see me," he replied, defeated.

"I think she doesn't know what world she is in at the moment. Go down to the shop, buy her some magazines, the trashier the better. It's what she needs right now. Get her some bits and I will go and talk to her but I won't tell her about this conversation. Go on, off you scoot."

George nodded silently and walked away, unconvinced.

The nurse made her way back into Sara's room, picking up the tissues from the main desk en route. Sara hadn't moved since she left her five minutes earlier. She was still on her left-hand side in an almost foetal position. Nurse Franklin knocked gently on the door.

"I said go away," Sara said in a tear-choked, nasal voice.

Nurse Franklin let herself in and pushed the door to.

"Not to me you didn't. I just want to check you're OK. It's not that often that we have a guy in here waiting day and night for three days for the woman he loves to come around and then when she does, she tells him to go away but she is the one crying. Well, I think if he didn't have to walk through a crowded hospital, he might've cried too, judging by his face. Do you want to tell me what's up?"

Sara sighed heavily. It was a prolonged sigh that seemed to have come from the bottom of her stomach.

"I only want to help," Nurse Franklin went on. "He has been in bits waiting for you, he loves you deeply and you are crying over him so you must feel something, too. You've been though a lot. Are you crying because of the attack?"

"No. Yes. I don't know."

"Well, that's a good start. It's completely normal to feel like that this soon after an attack like that. Why don't you want George around? He's completely smitten."

"Because I was just a job to him."

"A job?" the nurse echoed, bewildered.

Sara held a tissue to her nose and rubbed it a few times more than was necessary while she regained her composure. She lowered her arms to her sides and sat back and rested her head. She was tired. Weak. Upset.

"He was assigned to catch a hitman who was after me."

"A real hero, then?"

"No. I thought he met me and we fell in love. I was a job. He made me feel like we were together but obviously it was all part of the undercover operation."

"Oh, he definitely loves you. You have no reason to doubt that."

"Well, it's different now. If he had said from the minute we met what was going on, then maybe we could have had something but to live a secret life like that, I could never trust him. Worst of all, he should know that, based on where I have come from. I would live a miserable life not knowing when he was telling the truth or when he was lying so it's over. He's ruined what could have been great." She picked up her tissue again. "Because I really loved him." She began sobbing uncontrollably.

Nurse Franklin squeezed Sara's hand and offered a conflicted smile. She poured her a cup of water in one of those tiny white plastic cups from the Perspex jug on the bedside cabinet.

"Don't make permanent decisions based on temporary feelings. That would be my advice. Get some rest. Press the buzzer if you need me, sweetheart."

As the nurse left the room, George was walking towards her. They both stopped as they made eye contact and the nurse shook her head. George lowered his and turned around and left.

A few of the nurses were in the staff room having a five-minute breather. Nurse Franklin walked in and sighed before slumping into a chair.

"Someone needs a Quality Street. Amy, pass these to Chloë."

Nurse Chloë Franklin's deep train of thought was

interrupted by the big purple one hitting her in the face. "Oh, good shot," she said with a smile. It took her longer to open it than it did to eat it.

"What's up then, missus? One of your patients getting to you?'

"Yes, but not in the usual way. She's not dying any more. You know my girl in bed four? Well, she's come around and that guy who's been moping around after her for days, she's told him to clear off."

"Not that lovely big chap?" another of the nurses chimed in.

"Yeah. The copper."

"He's fair game, then?" Amy asked, bringing a chorus of tuts from the others.

"She's saying he only met her because he was doing an undercover operation. I think he sounds like a hero but she says she can't trust him. You can see they are both crazy about each other. It's like we are caught up in the middle of a film drama. Will they? Won't they? You know."

"Well I would." Amy scoffed some more chocolates.

"Yes, I think we had gathered that," Chloë retorted.

All the girls jumped to their feet when the sister walked into the room.

"Do you all need to be having a break at the same time?" she asked drily. The girls scattered like field mice who have seen a cat.

———

George reluctantly met Mel for lunch. He kidded himself it was because she needed support but he knew that, really, she wanted to know how he was.

He sat opposite her at a bistro table, poking his saucer about with his index finger. The saucer was supporting a cup of tea that had gone cold. They had covered the subject of Sara. Mel told him that she would come round and to give her some time. There was a brief moment of silence and he knew what was coming. The whole time he had been sitting by Sara's side, he had put Detective Chief Inspector Wilson in a box in his head and labelled it *grief* and closed the lid. He knew that any moment now he was going to come up in conversation and he was going to have to hold it together. The box didn't just contain grief. It was also harbouring a fair amount of guilt. Guilt that he hadn't given much thought to since the DCI's death. Guilt that he had put him in a box in his head until he knew Sara was OK. Guilt that he brought the case to the team. Guilt that he wasn't the one who was dead.

He began to visualise a tiny version of himself climbing inside his head, making his way along a dark hallway looking at labels on boxes he had stored over the years. *Dead wife*, *Dead father*, *More successful brother* were just a few of the recent ones he came across. As he continued to search, the noise of the café had disappeared completely. He passed *Not seeing Mum enough*, *Not going for that promotion*, *Kissing a woman at a Christmas party when I was still married* and he kept trundling along. The boxes had run out but he knew he had to keep going. They were all old boxes. He was looking for a new one. He felt his tiny self's legs slow down as if walking through water and he knew he was close now.

"George? George?" Mel clicked her fingers in front of his eyes. He lifted the lid of the box to open it. Whoosh. The water came out.

"Oh George, don't. You'll set me off."

He slapped the lid of the box back on and the tiny him ran away out of his imagination. He put his sleeves up to his eyes and mopped up the evidence of his emotional state.

"Sorry. I'm just tired."

"Don't act the bloody hard man. You've had a pretty shit week. Have you actually eaten? Don't answer that. I'm getting you a bacon butty and a sugary tea."

Mel got up and left him at the table to get him some food, which made him the happiest he had been in the last 24 hours. He pulled his phone out and looked at the screen. It showed the time and nothing else. No new message. Sara was gone. Suddenly the miniature him appeared again in his mind and started prising the box of grief back open.

"Sod off, you little git," he muttered to himself.

He blinked and the menace was gone. He took a deep breath and exhaled loudly and did the same again. Now he was ready to talk.

Mel sat back down, clutching a wooden spoon with a number on it. She grinned at him and he was glad he had met up with her after all. Mooching about alone and sad would have done him no good.

"So, what do we know, Mel. What's the latest?" George forced himself to raise the corners of his mouth in an attempt at a smile.

"Not a huge amount. They are going to speak to Sara today, now that she's awake. Maybe she will see you after that. She might feel down and be glad of a friendly face."

George raised his eyebrows and feigned another smile.

"Savic is in custody and is saying nothing. Standard. But here is the juicy bit and the bit that doesn't make much sense."

"I'm listening."

"Christian's wife was in Sara's house. Her name was Susan. That's who he killed at the door."

"What?" George furrowed his brow as theories began to crowd into his mind.

"Table 38?' the young waitress put down the bacon butty in front of Mel and the fry-up in front of George and walked off before she could be corrected. Mel swapped them around, along with the black coffee for her and the sweet tea for George.

"Fry-up? Really?" George mused.

"Yeah. I haven't eaten for days. I'm starving. You're still in shock and grieving. You'll be lucky to manage half of that butty. I'll take you for a fry-up in about 29 hours." She began tucking into her food and, if he hadn't taken her word for it, the speed she was going convinced him.

"Susan is Christian's wife and she was at the house?"

"Eat."

"And he stabbed her?"

"Eat."

"Why would he stab her? A warning to Sara? Did he think he would get away with it?"

"He didn't know he had done it." Mel shovelled in a big forkful of beans and tore off some toast with her teeth like a human terrier.

"What do you mean he didn't know he had done it?"

"Eat and talk, George. When he was questioned, he told them she drove him to it and that she had it coming to her. They questioned him further and asked him who he killed. He said Sara. They told him it was Susan and it was obviously news to him."

George was mid-mouthful and stopped chewing. His face said, "What?" for him. He continued to chew and shook his head. With a big gulp, he was able to say, "What?"

"Thought that was what you were trying to say."

"So Christian went to the house to kill Sara but killed Susan thinking it was Sara. Savic knew he was going there and had already made plans to go to mine, being one step ahead of us. DCI Wilson gets killed and Sara survives. You walked into my house, what did you see?"

"The boss was gone... almost. It was too late. Blood was spurting from his neck. Savic had fled the scene and Sara was injured but not dead. We found traces of Savic's blood in your hallway so the DCI must have put up a fight. We are hoping Sara will be able to tell us more." She picked up the tomato sauce and squeezed it all over the remains of her breakfast. "There was blood everywhere."

George watched as Mel continued to devour her breakfast, completely unaware of the imagery she was creating.

"You've got a stomach of steel, Mel."

CHAPTER NINETEEN

G eorge stood on the front doorstep of his house. His body was still as a statue as he held the key out in front of him just millimetres away from the lock. He kept it there for a moment as he imagined what he might see on the other side. A bloodstained carpet didn't bother him. The death of his boss was deeply painful for him but it was the thought of Sara defenceless against Savic that most affected him. He had failed her and for that he would never forgive himself.

He put the key back in his pocket and stepped backwards off the step. In his head, he heard Sara scream out for him. He shook it off and made his way to the back of the house. A big foot imprint in the flower bed captured his full attention. It was clearly a footprint belonging to a man and it was facing the back door. He looked at the large Roman-style fluted vase plant pot and tilted it to retrieve the backdoor key he always hid underneath. His stomach sank to the ground. The key was gone. Savic had got into the house because of him. Feeling helpless, he marched round to the front of the house, climbed into his car and drove to the nearest hotel. He needed different walls to stare at while he coped with the knowledge of his own negligence.

The immaculately uniformed eastern European front-of-house lady took George's booking. The name on her badge said she was called Anouska. He normally would have made some kind of polite conversation but his mind was reeling. Hundreds of images were flashing in front of his eyes and he felt as though he was flying down a helter-skelter that would never end.

Anouska went through the booking-in process. She asked him if he wanted to make a dinner reservation and he just about managed to shake his head. He couldn't speak. He couldn't focus his eyes. He knew now why Sara didn't want to see him. He had never lost control of his mind before but then he had never been this stupid before.

In a haze, he made his way to the lifts and almost collapsed into it as the doors opened. No one else was in it and so he slumped to the floor, rubbing his temples over and over.

The lift stopped and pinged. They were people on the other side this time but he pushed through them, keeping his eyes to the ground the whole time. Hurriedly, he swiped his room key and pushed his weight against the door to gain entry.

Immediately, he went to the minibar and took out all of the miniatures, then frantically opened them one by one and knocked them back. A whisky, a gin, a Bacardi, a bottle of white wine. He stopped at the red, hoping that small concoction would shut his brain up and let him have some rest. Leaving the discarded empties on the bed, he went into the fully tiled bathroom and turned on the modern rainforest-style shower. Quickly, the room was engulfed in steam. He stripped and gave himself up to the hot lashings of water on his skin. As the water rained down on his head and the alcohol swam through his veins, he visualised the stress oozing from his pores. He took a deep breath and exhaled slowly while counting, one... two...

three. His breathing was shaky. He took another breath and counted one... two... three... His breathing was getting steadier now. His heart had calmed and his head no longer felt as if it was preparing for take-off. He stepped out of the shower, careful not to slip on the wet floor tiles and wrapped himself up in the fluffiest of towels. It felt good on his skin and was the closest he'd had to a hug for a while. He only enjoyed the thought for a moment as it was quickly followed by his internal chatter telling him what a loser he was.

He went back into the bedroom, swiped the empties off the bed and picked up the remote. The screen had a personalised message just for him. "We hope you enjoy your stay, Mr Ramsay." It did nothing for him and he didn't see the point. He highlighted the radio option, selected Classic FM, lay down on the bed and began counting.

George woke to the room being a lot darker. He rubbed his eyes and looked at his watch. He'd been out for four hours. He sat upright and turned off the radio and put on the news. He called the restaurant and asked if he needed to reserve a table. They told him he didn't. Always a seat for one somewhere, he thought.

Getting up to fill the coffee machine with water, he picked up the phone that he had left face down on the side when he had arrived. Three missed calls from Mel and two messages. He called Mel back while picking up the empties from the floor and putting them in the bin.

"Mel? What's up?"

"Where have you been? I've been trying to get hold of you."

"I can see that. I've been asleep."

"Where?"

"I checked into a hotel. Look, I'm not in a great mood. What's up?"

"All right, cheery. Sara's interview. She's been

interviewed." She had George's attention now. "Fancy grabbing a bite to eat? Then I can fill you in." George felt his stomach lift about having a dinner companion.

"That would be good. I am at the Park Plaza. Meet me in the front lobby in half an hour?"

"Yeah, sure. Fancy."

"Oh actually, can I ask a favour?"

"Yeah, go for it."

"Can you swing by a store and pick me up a pack of boxers? Medium, please. And in that case, come to room four zero five but contain yourself."

"Ha. Of course I can. OK, be with you soon."

George hung up and got the one beer out of the fridge and a packet of crisps, disregarding the cost of these little in-room treasures.

CHAPTER TWENTY

M el used the distinctive police man's knock on the door and George answered in his robe. Mel came in and handed him a full carrier bag while trying not to look at him. They had worked together for years now but seeing a colleague in a dressing gown seemed too intimate to her. He thanked her and went into the bathroom, trying to avoid eye contact as well. He called out to her that she could have a drink from the minibar. Looking in the bag, he saw she had bought him boxers, socks, a T-shirt, a hoodie and a men's wash kit. He was impressed – he didn't know she was that thoughtful and it hadn't been long since they spoke on the phone.

Emerging in his new kit, he smiled at her. "Thanks, Mel. I'm impressed. You must have zoomed around the shop." He went to get his wallet.

"I already had the wash bag. It was a gift for my brother's birthday next week and the rest, well, I gathered you needed some clean bits. If you give me your sizes I can get you some more bits tomorrow. If I do that and the maids restock your minibar, you're sorted." George blushed. "It's OK. I don't blame you for emptying it. Come on, let's get some food. I'm starving." George nodded and handed her £50. Mel swept it into her bag and stood up. "I'm not joking. I'm ravenous. Let's go."

The restaurant was close to empty. George had clocked a lone man in the far corner, which put him at ease if he came back to dine on his own tomorrow. He wasn't afraid of dining alone – he just wished he could have Sara sitting opposite him.

Mel looked disappointed with the menu.

"What's the matter?"

"Well, look at it. Fois gras? Steak tartare? I just want a burger and chips or pizza or something."

"Let's ask the waiter." George suggested. "Drink?"

"No, thanks. Driving, George."

"Well I'm not so I will be indulging. Come on then, tell me about Sara," he said with a sigh.

The waiter came over and took their order. George was having a steak with beer and Mel settled for a stuffed chicken breast with potatoes and vegetables, swapping the potatoes for chips.

"Well. Not long after we left yours, she said that she and... well, they were just talking. She said the boss wasn't good at making conversation and it was awkward. She said she felt nervous, uneasy and just wanted the whole thing to be over. She said the house was quiet and the atmosphere was tense."

"Yes, and then what?" George was getting impatient.

"All right, George. I'm getting there. She said she felt as though she could sense a presence in the house but put it down to just being nervous. She said she went in to the kitchen and there was a knock at the front door. The boss went to answer it and she said it unfolded very quickly. She looked back into the living room and saw a struggle going on on the floor. She said she saw a flash of silver come up and then down, going into the

DCI's chest. She then said she ran out to the back garden and went to grab the spare key from under the pot plant. She had wanted to lock him in and get help. She knew that the guv'nor was not going to survive so she tried to escape. She was very emotional about not being able to help him. She had the key in her hand and was trying to lock the back door. She knew he had come in through the front but she said she knew he was after her and thought he would come through the back and had hoped the police would be at the front of the property. She said she thought this was all part of the undercover operation. Savic, who she has correctly identified, by the way, came out and she had no chance, really. He grabbed her and lifted her off the ground. She tried to fight back furiously. She hit him and punched him as much as she could, giving a gash to his face using the key she was holding. She had her blood on him and his DNA was on the key and her hand so there was no way he was getting away with it this time. He was the attacker all right. She bit him and he dropped her and she ran back into the house trying to make her escape but he caught her and stabbed her. She said she had to make a decision there and then whether to keep trying to run or pretend to die in front of him. She chose to play dead and prayed that he would leave. He did. He went to make a run for it and we arrived. The funny thing was, she was still clutching that key all the way to the hospital. The surgeon prised it from her hand and has handed it in to us.'

George put his beer down and leaned back. He felt an immense surge of pride. His girl, if she still was, was a fighter. She was tougher than he had given her credit for. He had pictured her being much more frightened and he would never have thought she would try and fight back. Not against someone like Savic. He smiled to himself at her bravery.

"Yeah, I wouldn't have thought it either. I thought she seemed like a bit of a wimp."

"Mel. Nicely."

"What? Well she is the absolute definition of girly."

"Or perhaps she's a dark horse."

The food arrived at the table and Mel had started tucking in before George could offer a toast to good health. He had raised his glass to Mel unnoticed but put it back down before she realised that she'd left him hanging.

"I've got to get her back. I don't understand why she won't talk to me. Could you talk to her for me? You're a woman." Mel looked up at him mid-mouthful and scowled. "You know what I mean. I'm a good guy. I love her and I don't know why she hates me."

"No." Mel's cheeks were so stuffed she looked like a hamster and her words were barely decipherable. "No way. I'm not getting involved. Ask one of the nurses to help you. Their job is to care. Mine is to kick arse." George observed Mel with a wry face and gracefully picked up his knife and fork, making sure his elbows were off the table.

Awhile later, George waved Mel off and made his way back to his room. He was going in happier than when he had arrived earlier that day. He felt like now he had a right to fight for Sara. While he had believed that his hidden key had left her vulnerable, he thought he could never face her again. Now, knowing that she used the key to fight with Savic and got his blood on it, he felt differently. He still felt ashamed for putting her at risk, he was in turmoil, but he had to see her to tell her how proud he was of her. Maybe she would let them be friends. That would be better than nothing, he told himself.

As he climbed into bed he wrote out a text: "I love you. Please speak to me soon. Goodnight xxxx."

CHAPTER TWENTY-ONE

The next morning, George woke up with a smile on his face, determination in his veins and a spring in his step. He was going to go to see Sara and try and get her to forgive him one more time. This called for a stop at a florist to pick up a decent bunch of flowers. He sprang out of bed, flicked the switch on the coffee machine and went into the bathroom and turned the shower on. He glided back into the bedroom and picked his coffee pod and put it in. He felt positive. Something told him today was going to be successful. It was that intuition he always had, it was back and he was going to act on it before it left him again.

Once ready, he checked the room, not really knowing what for as he patted his pockets to confirm he had everything on him that he needed. As he left the room, he pressed the "make up my room" button and breezed out of there as if he was on holiday and not staying at an hotel because his own house was a murder scene.

The reception desk gave him details of the nearest florist and he called them on his way there. He wanted big, bold and beautiful. A balloon as well for good measure. He had never really been one for big gestures but he needed to get his game on – this could be his last chance. The flower shop did him proud. The bouquet was beautiful even to him and he was not one for appreciating flowers. As he hopped back into his car a thought crossed his mind. It might be over the top? Too much? He told himself that he was doing it anyway. This was the last chance saloon.

A few streets away he pulled up outside Richards & Son jewellers. He ran in, knowing exactly what he wanted and was out of there again within 10 minutes, with a small velvet box tucked away in the inside pocket of his coat.

He arrived at the hospital feeling as if this were a job interview for his dream promotion and he had one chance to win, otherwise he would be miserable for ever. His heart was racing and his palms were sweaty. "Now or never," he muttered as he made his way into the building.

As he pushed through the double doors to the ward, he could see Sara had company and it looked as if they were packing up her things. He held the flowers in front of him so she wouldn't see his face. One of the nurses saw him and beamed at him.

"Is she leaving today?"

"Yes, you've caught her just in time."

"Who is that in there with her?"

"One of her friends. Louise, I think she said."

"OK, thanks."

Ignoring the terror raging inside of him that felt as if it was psychically eating his stomach, George entered the room and said hi to both of the girls. Sara looked at him and looked away. Louise said she would give them a minute and smiled sheepishly at George as she left the room.

"You're allowed home, then?"

"I'm not going back there. I'm going to Louise's."

"Sure. Sorry, that was a stupid thing to say. I can't go home, either." George sat there as Sara continued to pack her things and avoid him. He noticed that she seemed to be repacking her packing and knew she was deliberately delaying.

"Sara, please talk to me. I love you. I have fallen for you hook line and sinker and I can't bear to be without you. I'm sorry I couldn't protect you and I hate myself for it but if you would let me, I would protect you for the rest of my life. Here, I have something for you."

Sara's stomach flipped. Heat rushed to her head and she felt dizzy as she turned around and saw George extract a box from his pocket. She registered the size of it and felt disappointed that it wasn't a ring box.

George noticed her face change. He hadn't taken his eyes off her and he saw the flicker of disappointment which gave him a flicker of hope.

"It's not a ring." He laughed. "It's a bracelet. I wanted you to have something special after everything you've been through. It has the affinity symbol on it. It... it expresses my eternal love for you. Sorry it's not a ring but I didn't think you'd even take this, if I'm honest."

Sara sat on the edge of the bed and finally faced George. Here was a man who wanted to protect her. The last one wanted her dead. She did love him but she wasn't happy about the lies, but right now she had no one else offering to be her white knight. Perhaps he deserved a second chance – or at least the opportunity to explain.

"Thank you, George," she said, opening the box." It's beautiful. So are the flowers." George took the bracelet out of the box and put it on her wrist and then held her hand. She gently tried to tug it away but he pulled her in and he embraced her. She relaxed and hooked her arms around him. "God, I love you. Please be with me." Sara hugged him harder but said nothing. "At least come to my hotel and wash your hair. You smell like a hospital."

Sara laughed and then sucked her teeth. "Ouch."

"Sorry, I won't make you laugh again. Please come with me today. I've got a lovely hotel. You can have a hot bath, we can get room service or go to the restaurant if you feel up to it and we can talk. Nothing else. No expectations." Still holding her tightly and close to his chest, he heard a tiny, "OK," and a wave of ecstasy ran over his body.

George pressed the button for the barrier to raise for the underground parking at the hotel. Sara noticed that this wasn't a £35-a-night hotel. He was a man who liked his comforts, like Christian, she thought. She and George hadn't exchanged any chatter on the way there. Part of her was wishing she hadn't accepted his offer but the other, and slightly larger, part of her was craving him and tormenting herself over his lies.

George had almost broken the ice as many times as they had stopped at traffic lights but then he would stop himself in case he ruined it. She was with him and that was enough for now. He needed to get her to the hotel room and unwind. Perhaps they needn't speak about anything tonight at all. Perhaps they could just enjoy each other's company. George leapt out of the car and swiftly moved around to Sara's side to open the door, holding out a hooked arm for her to lean on. She looked up at him from the seat and paused before grabbing his elbow and accepting his help. He smiled and again stopped himself from saying anything. He opened the boot and picked up the bag of things that Louise had brought in and decided to break the ice with that as it wouldn't cause any upset.

"I'm glad you had a friend to bring some things in for you."

"What? A friend? I've got lots of friends. Of course,

someone was going to bring something in for me. God, do you think I'm that sad?"

George's stomach sank and he muttered, "Sorry, I meant..." and didn't bother finishing his sentence.

They made their way into the hotel and up to their room in silence. The reception staff raised their eyebrows at seeing him with his second female visitor in as many days but George didn't care about that. He just nodded and smiled at them as he continued to guide Sara through the lobby. The whole way back to the room, he wondered what he could say, how he could open the conversation and get them on track to a pleasant evening. His confidence and bravado that he had on his way to the hospital had deserted him.

They got into the room and he put Sara's bag on the bed. The two of them stood there as if in some kind of stand-off. He was the matador and she was the bull. He had no chance. She looked around the room and images of her with Christian flashed through her mind. All the times he swept her away on romantic weekends, always leaving her longing for more. She winced at the pain of his not wanting her. He didn't even want her alive. He wanted her dead. That still hadn't sunk in for her yet.

"I'm going for a bath." she told George, then turned her back on him and locked herself in the bathroom before he could say a word. His heart sank and he felt lost, helpless and redundant. He ran his hands through his hair, feeling desperate and frustrated. He leaned over to the small fridge of expensive treats and went to grab a beer before muttering, "Fuck it," and pushing the door closed. He leaned over to the bedside table on the other side of the bed and picked up the complimentary pen and scribbled on the notepad: "Gone to the bar." He stood up and decided to leave the moody lighting and the dark walls behind and try and think of what to do next over a beer with some natural light.

Sara examined her prune-like fingertips and decided it was time to get out of the bath now that the water had cooled and she was beginning to feel a chill. She pulled herself out and started to shake with the cold air. Picking up a big, fluffy five-star towel she wrapped it around her while looking at the scar that had been left on her body by Savic. It was a thick raised line, like a garden worm on her skin and the stitches made it look as if it was crawling through barbed wire. Christian would be with her for ever now, just not in the way she had wanted or ever expected. She cast her mind back to when they met, that fateful night in the bar. Who would ever have known that a stranger could take your heart and your mind in the way he had. How was she ever going to get over the fact he had wanted her dead. Her eyes pricked with tears and she leaned on the edge of the marble basin. "For fuck's sake," she said wiping her eyes and whimpering.

As Sara opened the bathroom door and watched the steam escape, she tried to send her feelings of despair with it. Gently putting one foot in front of the other she delicately moved forwards but was horrified to find she was alone. The walls began to press in and her heartbeat started to pound in her ears. She kept looking as if to see George but he wasn't there. There was no-where for him to hide. She wanted to scream. *How could he leave me alone like this?* The panic was increasing and she could feel her body shake. She pulled her bag off the bed tipping it upside down so that all the contents fell on the floor. She grabbed her phone and hit George's number. He answered after one ring and she screamed at him:

"Come back. Come back. Come back." She collapsed to the floor, clutching at her towel and sobbing heavily. George entered the room in a frenzy, running to Sara on the floor, kneeling beside her and taking her in his arms.

"My darling. What is it? What happened? I'm sorry. I'm so sorry."

Sara howled, sobbed and shook. She was distraught. Through her tears, she managed to mutter: "You left me alone. I was scared. I was so scared."

George held her close and felt even more of a fool than he had ever done up to this point.

The pair held on to each other on the floor of the hotel room. Sara felt better for having George holding her and came to realise that maybe she needed him more than she had thought. George held Sara, desperate to be her protector from now on. Her sobs became slower and her breathing began to steady. She had been face down on the floor with him cradling her but now she pulled herself up to a sitting position and nuzzled into his chest, still hiding her face from him. George breathed in the smell of her hair and kissed her head while holding her tightly. He kissed her head again and again and then tried to pull her face to his but she pulled back. He firmly brought her chin round her lips to his. She didn't kiss him back. He kissed her again but still no kiss back. "Sara, I love you so much." He kissed her again and this time she opened her mouth. They kissed with passion and intensity, like two wartime lovers being reunited.

Finally coming up for air, George held Sara's face in his hands. Deciding to move forwards he opted for no questions and told her to get ready for dinner. "The restaurant will be a good distraction and the food is great here." Sara pecked him on the lips and squeezed his hips. She got up and pulled her towel around her and began to pick her things up off the floor. George felt relieved. He felt hope for the first time since the stabbing.

Sara wore some casual jeans and pumps with a pretty

blouse. It was effortless but pretty. Her hair fell delicately around her neck. George had not watched her getting dressed. He was aware of the wall she had put up around herself but he was curious to see the wound. She sat on the edge of the bed, not saying a word.

"Ready?"

"Yes." She spoke in a very quiet voice and he hoped it wasn't embarrassment. He felt awful for scaring her like that but glad that he had benefited from it. If he hadn't gone to the bar, he suspected they wouldn't be going to dinner right now. He offered her his hand and she took it. Even the way she held his hand seemed weaker.

When they got down to the restaurant, Sara ordered a soft drink but George told the waiter to cancel it and bring her a glass of champagne. "Medicine," he told her, "and to celebrate your survival. In fact," he corrected himself, turning to the waiter, "make it a bottle." Her half-hearted smile told him she didn't feel like celebrating.

The popping of the cork broke what was becoming an uncomfortable silence for George. He was hoping the champagne might lighten the mood and get Sara to relax.

She took a big gulp and was ready for answers. "Why did you lie to me? That's the worst thing you could've done."

"I truly don't know what lies you're talking about."

"You're making it worse." She gulped down the rest of her glass. George picked up the bottle and poured her some more.

"I wanted to protect you. I should have told you at the first opportunity but it wasn't clear what the plan of action was immediately and the only thought I had was to protect you."

"Don't you think you could have done that by telling me?"

"Yes, and I was always going to tell you. I just, I just. Look Sara, I fell in love with you and it was unexpected. I didn't know how to tell you because I was scared you would run away."

Sara moved the glass, using her fingers at its base. She was staring intently at it and moved it around the linen tablecloth in a figure of eight. George felt as if nothing he could say would be the right thing in this awkward moment.

"Yes, but that's just it. You wouldn't have loved me if it hadn't been for this job and that's what bothers me the most."

"What? Sorry, I don't follow."

"I just think if you had met me first, it would have been different but knowing I was just a job makes me think you see me like some kind of damsel in distress and I don't like that. I didn't realise that's who you thought you were meeting."

"Sara, I am seriously confused," George said sincerely. "What are you talking about?"

"I just wish you met me first and fell in love with that Sara."

George stared at Sara in complete bewilderment. "Again, I'm not sure what you mean. I did meet you first. What?"

"You met me because you were watching Savic. I was part of the case. You didn't meet Sara. You met the target, the victim and then you pretended to want to be in a relationship with me to crack the case. That's what I can't stand. How long did you pretend before you felt it? You sucked me in and I believed you liked me for me."

George laughed and quickly stopped when he saw Sara's face. "Sara. I did meet you first. Is this what this has all been about? I met you at the doctor's surgery with my mum. You know that."

"Yes, but that was a set-up. That's what you people do. You knew I would be there and you made sure you were there and that was me entering the undercover operation. Was that woman even your mum or an actress?"

George started to laugh which increased to a bellowing. He leaned back in his chair and held his stomach.

Sara started to get rattled. "Stop laughing at me. Stop laughing at me now. This is not funny. You played me and that is what hurts."

George managed to calm himself down, still chuckling, and then looked at her square-on. "Sara, listen to me. I met you at the doctor's. That woman *is* my mother. We started dating and then, not long after, I spotted Savic near your house. He has been on our wanted list for years. I told the team and we began investigating. At that time, I had no idea he was after you."

Sara was dumbfounded. She stared at him and her eyes almost glazed over. George picked up her hands.

"Are you telling me you pushed me away because you thought this had been a set-up from the start?"

"Yes. That's exactly what I thought and I was devastated. I thought you had used me and were laughing at me."

"No. Never. Not once. So, now that you know that I did fall in love with the real you, what now?"

Sara blushed at how foolish she was feeling. "What do you mean what now?"

'Well, now that you know that I did fall in love with you for you, that I wasn't stalking you for the case, that our meeting at the doctor's was innocent, what now? Will you let me back in?"

Sheepishly, she managed to say: "Yes."

"Is that all you have to say? I was kind of hoping for a little more."

"Oh God, I'm sorry." She covered her face with her hands.

"Not an apology you, silly sod. Just something more romantic."

Sara pushed her chair back and got up out of her seat. She sat herself on George's lap and began to kiss him passionately. Their surroundings began to disappear as they locked mouths and held each other with their hands. Sara pulled away. "I love you. I love you very much." George pulled her face back to his and kissed her hard.

They were interrupted by their waiter who arrived and cleared his throat loudly. That was their cue to save their passion for the privacy of their bedroom.

One bottle of champagne, six oysters and a serving of halibut each later, the two of them had picked up where they left off on that fateful day. They had shared the right amount of hand-touching across the table, a good serving of laughs over dinner and a good handful of quiet moments where they looked into each other's eyes and said nothing.

They ordered a nightcap each to take to their room. A gin and tonic for her and a whisky on the rocks for him. George held his room key against the locking system on the bedroom door and pushed it open with his foot, ushering Sara forward before him.

She sat on the bed like a child being left with a new babysitter. George sat down next to her and told her he didn't want anything and that she could relax. He put his arm around her. He was like a mountain around her small frame. She handed him her drink and asked him to put it on the bedside table with his. When he turned back around, she was removing her top.

"Sara, don't. You know I don't want to push you."

"I thought you would want to see the wound." She held his gaze as she continued to pull her top over her head. She was sitting there in just her bra. It was such a pretty, feminine bra. Lilac and lacy with little flowers on it and then just above it was the big white waterproof dressing covering half of her chest. She began to peel from one corner and slowly lifted the edges. It was slow and sobering. She tugged it away and revealed a four-inch wound, aggressively stitched together. The stitches made it look worse. The idea that someone had penetrated her skin with a blade was bad enough for him to think about but for some reason, the idea of a needle being woven in and out of her flesh to repair her made her seem to him even more butchered. She picked up his hand and traced his fingers over it gently. He kissed her around it and then on gently kissed her on the top of her head. Leaning down to the floor, he picked up a new dressing that was lying there from the strewn items earlier. He carefully removed it from its sterile packaging and delicately placed it on to her body, gently running his index finger around the edge ensuring the glue was stuck firmly to her skin. He kissed her on the head again.

Sara leaned forward to get her top but ended up undoing her jeans. George looked at her helplessly. She looked at him and bit her lip. He bit his lip in return. She slipped her jeans off and asked him to unhook her bra. He kissed her back as he did it. Then she sat down next to him and moved her head towards his lips. George hesitated then stood up and scooped her into his arms before laying her down on the bed. He started kissing her neck and saw the goose bumps rise on her body. The heat rushed to his groin and his heart raced as she began to undo his belt. He pulled at her small silk pants and slid them down her legs.

As he lowered himself on top of her, she gasped and he held himself still.

"Are you OK?" he asked anxiously.

"I'm more than OK," she replied.

They kissed and made tender, gentle, real love in the dim light of the bedside lamp.

CHAPTER TWENTY-TWO

The next morning George and Sara woke up in each other's arms. George had woken before Sara and had enjoyed the quiet time where she was oblivious to him adoring her and the delight he was feeling that she was back in his arms. The navy wall décor teamed with a gold dado rail and the black-out curtains offered not much more than a silhouette of her body. There was a small gap between the curtains, allowing a sliver of sunlight into the room that highlighted her curves as she lay naked next to him, only half-covered with the duvet. In the beam of light that came in, he could see tiny dust particles floating down as he drew on her back with his index finger.

Slowly she stirred and rolled over to him, wincing at the pain from her wound. He sat upright immediately and attempted to help but then quickly withdrew. He knew she would want to pull herself up. She was injured. She wasn't a broken doll. She managed to get to a sitting position and rested her head on his shoulder. He put his arm around her and stroked her skin gently. The pair of them sat there quietly for a few minutes both equally enjoying the moment. Both were smiling without knowing the other one was smiling.

"Are you OK, after last night? We should have waited." George stroked her arm very gently, admiring her baby-soft skin.

"I wanted to. Don't worry. I feel all right." She lay in to his cuddle harder.

"Coffee?" He kissed her temple and was about to get up.

"In a minute. Just sit with me for a little longer." She closed her eyes and enjoyed his embrace. George pulled her in tighter in agreement. "I had a really lovely time last night. I feel loved with you and I need that. It completes me. Makes me a better person, you know?"

"I know, darling. I know exactly."

"I love you, too, by the way. What I mean is, it's so good to both be in love with each other. I'm going to shut up before I say too much."

"It's OK. I know I'm not your first love, I just want to be your last."

She smiled at him and he leaned down and kissed her on the lips. A lingering, soft, gentle kiss. George then eased himself away and got out of bed to make the coffee. All the while, the pair of them continued to exchange smiles and took it in turns to blush.

Sara leaned back on the bed and felt surprisingly comfortable. This wasn't her house, she didn't want to be there. It wasn't his house, she didn't want to be there, either. This was a bolt-hole that she wouldn't have agreed to 36 hours ago but it was exactly the right thing to do. If she had gone to Louise's, she would want to ask question after question about what happened and she would undoubtedly give opinion after opinion about what Sara should do next.

When Sara agreed to go with George, it was just to buy

herself some time to decide what to do. She wanted some head space before her parents got the chance to look after her. She knew George wouldn't push her or ask too much. She knew they could easily pass the evening away and now she was glad she had. That bit, she had got right, whereas everything else she had thought about him recently, she had got completely wrong.

Everything that she had been upset about had been all wrong. He was still the perfect man she had been waiting for.

"Why don't we just chill today. The hotel has a spa. We could use that. Book yourself in for a treatment perhaps?"

"I don't want to be without you. Not yet." She pulled her knees up to her chest and hooked her arms around them. She looked like a defenceless child again, one that needed his protection.

"Of course, honey. I will be right by your side as long as you need me to be. I'm not going anywhere. We can sit in here all day with the curtains closed, if you like."

"No, I think we should do something. Maybe go and use the pool and head out for lunch? I've got to try and act like everything is normal. I just don't want to be locked in a treatment room alone with a stranger but we should do something. I have to make some effort."

"They chinked coffee cups and smiled at each other. George joined her on the bed and aimed the remote control at the television. Sara nuzzled back into his chest again. They were both exactly where they wanted to be.

A cup of coffee and a programme about antiques on television later, Sara was ready to face the day. She picked up her bag from the floor when it occurred to her that she didn't have any swimwear. George saw her face.

"What's up, honey?"

"Oh, it's nothing. I just don't have any swimwear with me."

"OK. Well, let's go out and get you some."

"I don't know. I don't really want to go out just yet."

"But you don't want to stay in the room, either. Hang on, I have an idea." George picked up the phone and called reception. They put him through to the spa who confirmed they sold swimwear. "Sorted. We can get you something down there."

Sara relaxed her shoulders and smiled at George. She walked over to him and wrapped her arms around his waist. "You think of everything, don't you?"

"I just wanted to be able to help you leave the room but not have to leave the hotel. I would have paid the concierge to go out and get you something otherwise."

She gently slapped his chest. "You would not. I wouldn't have allowed it."

"You couldn't stop me when it comes to trying to make you happy. Shall we go to the pool now, then?"

Sara put on the robe and complimentary slippers and passed the other pair to George. For a moment, she almost forgot why they were here. She felt as though she could be on holiday. The posh room, the coffees in bed, the five-star dining and now a visit to the pool. The other residents would think they were a couple in love having a romantic break. No one would suspect he was a police officer resting after a major case that cost the life of his boss and no one would believe that Sara had been stabbed by one of the country's most wanted men – and survived.

George was looking through the bikinis on wire hangers and was about to suggest one when he saw Sara looking at one-pieces. It occurred to him that she must be feeling self-conscious and didn't want anyone to see her wound.

"Have you found one you like? We can just bill it to the room."

Sara was feeling the fabric between her fingers and looking

crestfallen. "I can't go swimming. What with my dressing. I wasn't thinking." She looked fed up.

"OK, here's what we'll do. Let's go back to the room. Let's get dressed. Dress up for a date and we will go out for lunch. I know you don't want to but we'll be fine. We can get a taxi from here to the restaurant door and a taxi back. No walking about in crowds with strangers, OK? We will be safe. Trust me."

"I don't want to but I do trust you so, OK, let's do it."

George took Sara by the hand and they walked back to their room, slowly. George wanted to savour every moment and was taking his role of protector very seriously.

Sara didn't really have the clothes with her that she would class as date standard but she worked with what she had. Louise had packed her a few blouses and some heels so she was able to go smart casual. She put a bit more make-up on than usual but felt a hundred pounds rather than a million dollars.

She looked at George, who was wearing jeans and a long-sleeved shirt tucked in with some suede ankle-boots. He was effortlessly stylish. He would say he wasn't one for fashion but he got it right when it came to dressing himself. No embarrassing-dad hiking trainers or a T-shirt with a cringe-making slogan on it. He had classic staple items and always seemed well turned out. As Sara took in the view, it was as if she physically felt her heart soften. As if it was unfolding in her chest like a piece of crumpled up paper. Something felt different now. Before the attack, they were two new lovers where everything was exciting and uncertain but now, it seemed to her that everything was calm. At least, she felt calm. The butterflies were still there but now it was as though they danced around continuously in her tummy. Before the stabbing, the butterflies were a nervous flurry telling her that she had something so good she was afraid to lose it. The relationship seemed more secure now. She winced at how close she had been to giving it all up based on a belief that simply wasn't true.

They left the room and George held her hand tightly through the hotel and into the lobby and then out into one of the waiting taxis. He didn't let go until he had to open the door for her which he then held and closed it once she was strapped in. He walked around the other side, got in next to her, clipped himself in and put his hand on her knee. She might have felt smothered if this had been someone else but right now, it was exactly what she wanted.

True to his word, they pulled up outside a restaurant. It was a back-street, intimate Italian place. He got out and, once again, walked around to her side. The taxi driver was about to pip him to the post but George politely told him he could do it and handed him a note which was much more than the cost of the ride. Sara observed it and felt a warm glow that she had one of the good guys. Her dad had always told her to look for a man who tips well. George helped his hesitant girlfriend get out of the taxi and ushered her in without giving her much chance to think about it. They were seated immediately and George ordered a bottle of wine and a jug of tap water with ice and lemon slices.

"See? We did it. You did it."

Sara smiled softly. "We did. Here we are. My first outing since the day I was stabbed."

"Do you really want to think of that? We can talk about it if you like. I just thought it might be a bit soon."

"I guess. Let's leave it. I'm starving. That has to be a good thing, right?"

"It certainly is. I know what I'm having. Cheesy garlic bread to start so you might want to order something similar so we can both reek."

"I quite fancy some arancini but I'll gladly have a bite of your bread."

"Only if I can have a bite of your balls?"

"Shouldn't that be the other way around?" They both giggled and grinned at each other just as the waiter was pouring their wine.

"A toast?" Suggested George.

"To?"

"To smooth sailing."

Sara raised her glass and clinked his. "To smooth sailing."

CHAPTER TWENTY-THREE

L ater that day, back at the hotel, Sara began to pack up her belongings and said that her parents were coming to collect her. They had wanted to see her for days but she had told them she wanted some alone time with George. She couldn't live in a hotel for ever and she didn't want to go back to her house, even if she were allowed to, so she was going to have to move back home for a while. It wasn't ideal. She had lived on her own for a few years and as much as it would be lovely to be wrapped up in cotton wool for a few days, she suspected it would soon become suffocating.

George was being very quiet. She could sense he wanted her to stay but they both knew that wasn't an option.

"Why don't you invite your parents into the hotel for dinner? I'd like to meet them." That was the best George could think of to get some more of her time.

"You want to have dinner with my parents?" Sara looked at him as if he were crazy while she folded up a blouse.

"Well, I have to meet them at some point and now seems as

good a time as any to me. If I'm honest, I'd like them to know that you have someone who wants to protect you."

Sara moved around nervously, trying to find something to do but realising there was no getting out of it. "Yeah, OK, I'll send them a text."

George got up and put his arms around her waist. Sara looked up at him, her eyes big and shining. He could see his own reflection in her pupils. He watched them dilate in front of him and suddenly they were kissing passionately and taking their clothes off. He picked her up and gently lowered her on to the bed. She never took her eyes off him as he kissed her with his eyes open. Leaning on one elbow, he ran his fingers through her hair. The desire between them was intense as the material world around them began to dissolve and they were suddenly in their own universe. As their bodies rocked together in unison, his back became wet with sweat. She held him tighter, squeezing his arms and letting him know that she was there. He shuddered at the same time as her legs began to shake and they both locked eyes as he told her... "Yes, yes, yes." His body gave three sharp thrusts and she pulled his hair and arched her back. He kissed her clammy chest and rolled off her as carefully as he could and lay next to her, pulling her into a cuddle. Their chests were rising quickly and in unison. Sara ran her fingers over his chest.

"Wow."

"I agree." Silence. "Sara, don't go. I don't want you to go now that I've got you back."

"We can't live in a hotel, George. And neither of us can go home, either."

"Well, how about we rent a place together. We could put both our houses on the market and then buy something together."

Sara's heart began to flutter. "Do you really want to do that?"

"I want nothing more."

"Maybe we could stay at my parents' until we can find a rental? It could take a couple of weeks."

"No offence but I'd rather stay here. I would feel awkward, given that we haven't actually met yet."

"I can appreciate that. You can't stay here – it will cost a fortune."

"OK, how about we stay here tonight and then we could look on line for a holiday let, a self-contained flat or something, that we could use until we can move in somewhere?"

"I would love that." She rolled round to look at him and her whole face had lit up. She was very excited and he was just as elated to see it. "My parents will have something to say about it, I suspect, but I will deal with them. Oh my God, I'm so excited."

"So am I, babe. So am I."

———

The evening couldn't have gone better. It began with the obligatory onslaught of questions from Sara's parents, which of course they tried to pretend they were asking on the spur of the moment and hadn't given much thought to what had happened. George answered everything perfectly. Sara's mother, Ruth, was itching to know the details of the case. Knowing that Sara was safe from harm, her concerns had been pushed to the side and she was now indiscreetly delving for information. Sara's dad, Alan, was a bit more polite and tutted at each probing question. Ruth made a big play of how offended she was at her husband's disapproval, which made Alan sigh with despair. Sara in turn rolled her eyes at George, so George told them it was honestly fine and he would answer anything he was allowed to.

Once the fascination with his job was over and the enquiries stopped coming, the table began to relax and Ruth finally asked Sara: "How are you in yourself?"

"I'm fine Mum, honest. In fact, we have something to tell you."

"Oh, you're not pregnant, are you?" Ruth was holding her glass mid-air waiting for her response.

"Oh, for heaven's sake Ruth, let the girl speak." Some might have said Alan was cross but this is how they were together and had been as long as Sara could remember.

"No, mother, I am not pregnant. George and I are going to move in together. I don't want to go back to mine, he doesn't want to go back to his but we do want to be together and support each other through this. So, I won't be coming back with you tonight. I hope you will understand."

Ruth looked at Sara and then looked at George and then back at Sara.

"Well, if it's what you want, I can understand that. But you could've told me before I made up the bed."

George lowered his eyes in amazement at how self-centred Ruth's comment sounded. He could tell she wasn't malicious but just completely unaware of how she came across. Alan broke the silence.

"Don't worry about that. I might be sleeping in there yet."

Sara giggled and George gave Alan a knowing look.

"Don't give me your sympathy, son, you've got all this to come." The men chinked glasses and the whole table laughed.

The drinks flowed easily and the group seemed to bond well. Occasionally George would put his hand on Sara's knee under the table or his arm around her shoulders. Not so much that it would show her parents a lack of respect but enough to show them he cared.

By the end of the evening, Ruth had relaxed and seemed a bit taken with George herself. The men fought over the bill but Alan won, saying that it was the least they could do after everything that had happened.

"By the sound of it, there will be plenty of occasions for you to return the favour. Anyway, in all seriousness, thank you, George. I can sleep a bit better now knowing Sara has got a good man in her life." He gave George a firm handshake.

"I won't let any of you down." George cupped Alan's hand.

Ruth kissed and hugged her daughter goodbye, her eyes shiny with tears.

"Don't cry, Mum."

"We almost lost you. You're still my baby, Sara."

"I know, I know." She pulled her mum in close and they shared a very deeply felt hug.

George and Sara waved her parents off, satisfied and secure with their daughter's future.

"Shall we go to the bar for a nightcap? Make the most of our 'holiday'?" George winked at his girl.

"Yes, OK, let's." She smiled up at him and she wasn't sure if it was the alcohol or a physical sensation of adoration running through her veins.

Over a large gin and tonic, they revelled in what a success the evening had been and began excitedly talking about what would happen next. They looked on some rental websites to see what was available and found there were loads of flats. Finding something to settle into soon shouldn't be a problem. They simultaneously put their glasses down and decided to call it a night.

As they walked away from the bar area, Sara heard what sounded like footsteps running up behind her. She turned around and her world seemed to go into a blur. A teenager in black jeans and a hooded jumper was lunging at her, wielding a blade. Everything slowed down and the noise drowned out. In her peripheral vision, she saw a waiter throw a tray of drinks up in the air. Suddenly the movement went back to real time and the boy shouted: "You ruined my fucking life, you whore." He lifted the blade up in the air and she froze to the spot. George pounced on the youngster who brought the knife down and into George's back. Sara gasped in horror as George wrestled with the boy who was still desperately trying to attack. He managed to get the teenager off him and on to his back. The boy was still clutching on to the knife, jabbing and lunging and not giving up. George battled with him, forcing the blade away from him and down. Suddenly, the youth's strength failed and George's weight plunged the knife into his chest. The boy's eyes changed, glazing. He fell backwards and George slowly got to his feet. Blood spluttered out of the boy's mouth and then George collapsed to the floor.

Sara shrieked blood-curdling screams. People began to appear. Sara was kneeling on the ground, trying to keep George awake.

"Call an ambulance. Call a fucking ambulance. Stay with me, George. Please, please don't go. I need you so much."

CHAPTER TWENTY-FOUR

A s the horror unfolded once again in front of Sara's eyes, her vision seemed to become pixelated. It was as if she was looking out of a frosted-glass window. She could make out the bodies slumped on the floor. The pool of blood on the floor. The flashing blue lights outside by the hotel entrance. The staff were milling about and the emergency services were moving around in front of her like thick strokes of paint on an impressionist canvas.

George and the attacker were lifted and strapped into stretchers and Sara was taken by the arm and guided away from the scene and into the back of the ambulance by she didn't know who.

"Please stay with me. Don't go now." She looked up above her and whispered: "Haven't we been through enough?' The tears rolled down her cheeks, taking her mascara with them.

The bright lights hurt her eyes as the commotion played out in an exaggerated speed in front of her. She couldn't bring herself to look at George, she didn't want to make an assumption. Turning her back on the paramedic in charge and hands clasped, she prayed over and over again in her head for a miracle.

Suddenly they were outside the accident and emergency department. The back doors were flung open and the dark evening made everything seem more sombre and more real. The stretcher was hurriedly wheeled out and the awaiting team pounced and took over.

"Come with me and I'll take you to the family room. We will do everything we can."

Saliva filled Sara's mouth and she was only given one stomach lurch as a warning before she threw up on the floor in front of her. Apologetically, she looked at the nurse as she placed her hand over her mouth.

"Don't you dare apologise. Someone will clean that up, you just come with me. Stephen. Clean-up needed over here. Thanks." She walked with Sara who recognised the surroundings she had left only 48 hours earlier. The nurse had tried to talk to her all the way down the corridor but she couldn't take in the words that were being said. This was all too much. She was overwhelmed with what-ifs. She wanted George in her life, she needed George in her life. The panic that consumed her made her want to scream out and wail but she tried to hold it all in, only allowing sporadic whimpers to escape from her mouth.

She sat down on the same sofa where George had sat waiting for her not so long ago. The nurse had gone to get her a cup of tea. As she took in her surroundings and made observations she wondered what George had thought of the room and if it was the same as the thoughts she was having now. She wondered if he had felt as scared as she had and guilt crept in about how she shunned him when she came to. She would always feel awful about that now.

The time that passed was excruciating as Sara prepared

herself for the worst and wondered what that would mean for her life from here on. She would have nothing. Her life as she knew it just a couple of weeks ago was gone. She would have to start from scratch and she didn't think she had the energy nor the desire to do that. She wanted to crawl into a dark hole and never face daylight again. For a small moment, she wondered if she could go through with suicide and then she pictured her parents and knew she would have to stay for them.

About an hour or so later, the door opened and the bright strip lights of the hospital department let in hopeful light into the subdued dusky pink room.

"Miss Edgerton, it's good news. He's going to be OK. Although he has suffered several stab wounds, none of them hit any vital organ. He is going to need some rest so he'll be with us for a few days, I suspect. He's still in recovery at the moment but he will be ready to see you in a short while."

The floodgates opened. A tsunami of emotion escaped from Sara's core and she almost collapsed to the floor. She sobbed and took a few deep breaths and stood up to hug the nurse.

"Thank you so much. I was so scared. I just couldn't even..."

"Shh, you don't need to think like that now. He's going to be OK. The police have been hanging around. Do you think you will be OK to talk to them? I've told them they can't see George until tomorrow."

"Yes, I can talk to them. Thanks."

The nurse smiled and left the room and Sara felt as if she could do a little dance if she wasn't still recovering from her own stab wound. She looked up to the ceiling and mouthed "thank you" and then two police officers came in.

Sara spent the next 45 minutes explaining what she could. Most of the information she gave them was about before the attack. The attack itself was sudden and chaotic. She relived the moments of happiness as her parents gave George their approval and her excitement about making plans to move in with George. They had been so happy and then terror struck without warning. She hadn't even seen the boy. George had seen him first and rushed to her defence. Her true hero. They grappled and there was blood but she didn't know who from. Several staff members appeared from nowhere trying to help and pin down the young man. The blue lights seemed to have appeared very quickly, for which she would be eternally grateful, and the only other thing she could add was that she thought it must have been one of Christian's children. The way he called her a bitch and said she had ruined his life. It couldn't be anyone else. The police thanked her for her time and closed their notebooks. They said she had been very helpful and to pass on their best to George and that they hoped to see him back to work soon.

As they left the room the kind nurse gave her a nod which said she could come and see him.

"Weren't you in here just a few days ago?"

"I was, yeah. But sorry, I don't recognise you."

"I was with other patients but I recognised your face. You two have been through the mill. Upwards from here, eh?"

"I really hope so."

George was lying in his bed with his covers up to his waist. He had three dressings on his torso in different areas.

"You were so lucky. I can't believe I almost lost you."

"Your idea of lucky is different from mine.," he replied with a chuckle.

"Always making jokes! Take it easy and don't overdo it. It's my turn to look after you now."

"I like the sound of that."

She kissed him on the head and held his hand. "Try to get some sleep, it's late. I'm not going anywhere."

Sara's parents were devastated to learn that they had left moments before the next nightmare unfolded. Sara's father even remembered seeing a young man in a hooded jumper entering the hotel as they drove off. They insisted she come to stay with them until she got back on her feet and that George would join her as soon as he was released. Sara's mum went back to the hotel with her and helped pack up their things and she settled the room bill in George's absence. Sara knew George would pay it back immediately. She just needed to tie up these loose ends and get back to a place of safety.

The police confirmed that the attacker had been Christian's son. They also confirmed that he did not make it. He was 15, not even an adult. The police said no charges would be brought over his death as George had clearly acted in self-defence. There would still be an official process but, based on the events as they happened, they wanted to reassure George that once the formalities had taken place, he would not be held responsible for the young man's death. Although that was a relief, it was desperately sad for everyone involved. Sara tried not to think of the remaining son. Orphaned and now without his brother. All of this damage because of a love affair.

A few days had passed and George was allowed to leave. Sara's mother was, if anything, more excited than she was. She was very keen to have them both home and give them hot food and shelter. She was thrilled to have them under her roof and play the homemaker for them, however briefly it might be.

George was sitting up on his bed with the bag of things that Sara had brought in for him. The image of him sitting there and knowing he was hers made her feel warm. She was ashamed to know that it took her almost losing her life to see him for who he was. She hadn't realised her barriers were up that high and wondered whether, if Christian hadn't tried to have her killed, they would have ever developed further than they had before the incident. It was a strange feeling to know that Christian actually helped her to move on by trying to have her killed. It was bittersweet.

"Hey soldier, ready to move in to the in-laws?" Sara noticed George tense up. "Sorry, too soon? We can get out of there as quickly as we like. I know it's not ideal but don't feel awkward. Mum is super-excited and I think Dad is looking forward to your company too."

"I'm fine, honestly and I don't want you to think I'm ungrateful. It's just that I *do* feel awkward. I only met them a few nights ago and I was telling them I was going to look after you and now they are looking after me. In fact, now that I think about it, I have failed you all." George looked down and Sara got the distinct impression he was about to cry. She sat on the bed next to him, put her arm around him and rested her head on his shoulder.

"You haven't let anyone down, you nutter. You saved everyone and it almost cost you your own life."

George waved his hand dismissively. He was still looking down. Sara could see he was struggling.

"Baby, you are coping with a lot right now. Please don't feel down on yourself. Let's go and get a change of scene. Dad is waiting outside."

"He died, Sara," George managed to say in a choked voice. "He was 15 and I killed him." Now the tears from George came. Sara hugged him hard and cried with him.

"This is not your fault."

CHAPTER TWENTY-FIVE

Sara and George settled in quite comfortably at her parents' house. Any fears they might have had came to nothing. Sara contemplated the fact that again, probably the horror they had been subjected to over the last few weeks had made this situation so easy. She couldn't have moved back home complete with new boyfriend in tow – one whom her parents hardly even knew – under any other circumstances. Once more, she found herself thinking that, yet again, Christian had in a way caused this situation. What he set out to do had resulted in a completely opposite outcome. She had survived. Her parents loved George. They were all staying under one roof and all happy to be doing so.

Sara's mum delighted in having to cook for lots of people and her dad enjoyed not being outnumbered. He and George even took to sharing a couple of beers whilst watching sport together. Sara's dad had Sky Television only for the sport. He had all the channels and he didn't care what it was or who was playing, if he could have sport on the television, he would. Sara also got the impression that George was beginning to feel as if he belonged somewhere and although they hadn't spoken about his dad much, she began to see that he liked the role of son-in-law.

Sara and George didn't have to lift a finger. All of their meals were cooked. Every drink was made and handed to them with care. Clean, soft towels were provided every day. As it was getting so close to Christmas, Sara's parents were trying to convince them to stay until the new year, at least. Although it hadn't been in their plan, they could see that it was beginning to make sense.

That night, Sara and George lay in bed together. Sara was on her back and George was on his side facing her and tracing his fingertips over her skin.

"Do you think they are listening in?"

"Probably." She started to giggle quietly.

"If we stay here until the new year, does that mean that I can't make love to you until we move?"

"George." She picked up a cushion and gently hit him on the head with it.

"Well, I am only human and you are gorgeous."

"I'm sure we can find an opportunity. You're not well enough yet, anyway."

"Ahem, I think I will be the judge of that," George argued. "Plus, you were all over me when you came out of hospital. I've been out for three days now and my injuries weren't as bad as yours."

"I'm scared I'll hurt you."

"Kiss me."

In the bedroom next door, Sara's parents were sitting up with a book each and a lamp on each bedside table alight. Ruth put her book down.

"I'm so glad they are here, aren't you?" She looked over to

her husband when they heard Sara laugh and telling George to be quiet. Alan looked at his wife and raised an eyebrow.

"I'm going downstairs."

"Good idea, love. Me too."

They both crept out and went down for a mug of Horlicks.

Sara and George stopped in their tracks as they heard her parents making their way downstairs. George was hovering over Sara, supported only by his elbows and they both locked eyes and clenched teeth. He then slowly and tantalisingly started kissing her neck. She rolled over and pushed him on to his back.

"You are too wounded for this. Let me take the lead."

"That, I like the sound of."

———

Breakfast the following morning in the Edgerton residence had a different atmosphere. Sara and George felt as though they were on eggshells. Alan didn't know where to look and Ruth was the most relaxed. She remembered being Sara's age and she was still ecstatic to have her home.

Sara nonchalantly greeted both her parents and tried her best to be bright and breezy. Alan gave her a nod and took his coffee and his paper into the living room. Sara felt a slight tug of unease in her tummy.

"What's for breakfast, mum?"

"Eggs? How would you like them? Fertilised?"

Sara's face flooded with a shade of crimson and her mum laughed.

"These walls don't hold any secrets, I'm afraid, love. You're not a young girl any more, I have to accept that."

"Mum, can we please talk about something else. George is going to be so embarrassed."

"Your dad and I are going to go out for some dinner tonight so you two can have some alone time. How does that sound?"

"Sounds pretty good, actually. Thanks, Mum."

Ruth winked at Sara, who blushed again. George and Alan were sitting silently in the front room. The news was on but it was unclear as to whether either of them was actually listening to it. George's phone rang. He stood up and went into the kitchen to take the call. Sara couldn't really make out what was being said but it sounded like it might be his work.

"Who is that he's talking to?" Ruth couldn't contain her curiosity.

"I thought this house held no secrets?" Sara glared at her mum while Alan cleared his throat. "It sounds like it's his work. They probably want to talk to him about what happened. He hasn't given an official statement yet."

George came back into the living room with the phone still in his hand.

"That was work. They want me to go in and give a statement."

"OK, babe. Do you want me to come with you?" Sara stood up and held his hand.

"No, there's no need. You won't be able to come into the interview room with me and God knows how long I will be." He gave her small hand a brief squeeze in his large one.

Alan looked up from his paper.

"Do you want a lift to the station, son?"

George and Sara both looked at each other and smiled.

"Thanks, Alan. That would be great."

CHAPTER TWENTY-SIX

Sara and Ruth hadn't spent a day together in such a long time. Ruth had asked her if she wanted to go out and do something but they both knew she didn't. It was a cold and gloomy November day. Sara wanted to stay in and suggested they watch a film together and maybe bake a cake for the men. Ruth thought that was a splendid idea.

Sara tuned into the daytime television while Ruth went and had a shower first. She sat on the armchair with her feet curled up beneath her and took a moment to appreciate it, how nice it felt to not have to do anything. She wasn't expected in at work. She didn't have to clean her house or do any washing. She didn't even have to make herself a cup of tea if she didn't want to. All of those menial tasks that don't require much but are so nice to have someone to do them for you. She kept looking at her phone for an update knowing there wouldn't be one. He'd be gone for hours.

She had various texts from friends asking how she was, checking in on her. She had sent a blanket text back saying she was fine but not up to seeing anyone at the moment. She knew they meant well but they would revel in the drama of it all and she was still recovering from the horror she had lived through. Every time she closed her eyes, she could see Savic with his ice-cold death stare looking at her. She shuddered and got goose pimples at the thought. She told herself to stop drifting off and watch the television. There was a competition to win a holiday for two to Barbados and £50,000 pounds. She picked up her phone and wrote out the text WIN in capital letters as the presenter instructed. She typed in the number to send it to and off it went. She got an immediate response telling her an entry had been placed and that she could have another one for £2. She ignored it and changed the channel telling herself that no one ever wins those things, really.

Shortly afterwards, Ruth appeared, dressed but with wet hair and no make-up on.

"What kind of baking do you want to do, then? One big cake or a batch of cupcakes?"

"I think carrot cake for Dad and maybe some cupcakes, too?"

Sara had always been an excellent baker. Most of her childhood weekends had been spent baking with her mum. When she started secondary school, she was without a doubt the best baker in her class. She wasn't so great with the savoury stuff but she took a real pride in cakes and her presentation of them was outstanding. The way she decorated them was art. Her parents and teachers thought she would go professional but she had never planned for that and had just enjoyed doing it to relax. When she took her first office job, her mum was slightly disappointed and asked her why she didn't want to make a career out something she was so good at and clearly loved. Sara replied: "Because I do love it so much. It's my escape. How can I get away from the everyday if I make this my everyday?" Ruth understood completely.

Once out of education, Sara very rarely baked so Ruth was delighted that they would be doing it together today. Her daughter needed some distraction and she was going to help her. Ruth needed to feel needed so they were complementing each other perfectly. Sara had grown up so quickly and Ruth had struggled with her slipping away as she got older. She was always going out with friends for lunch or nights out or concerts and Ruth didn't seem to get a look-in. She never told Sara how discarded she felt, she knew she had to let her fly but it still smarted a bit.

Ruth got out the mixing bowls and a whisk. She unhooked her apron from the back of the kitchen door and wrapped it around herself. It was emblazoned with an image of Miss Piggy and the words *Pretentious? Moi?* Alan had bought it for her a few Christmases ago and thought it was funny. Ruth didn't.

Sara decided there was no point in getting dressed and showered until she had finished baking. She swept up her glossy blonde hair into a messy bun and said she was ready. Ruth looked at her daughter and was amazed at how she could make a pair of tartan pyjama bottoms and a black vest with bed hair look so cool and stylish. But Sara did. She always did.

About an hour later, the kitchen looked as if a flour bomb had gone off and Sara said she was going to get showered while the cakes were in the oven. She loaded the dishwasher, gave her mum a kiss on the cheek and skipped upstairs.

Today, Sara felt the best she had for a while. She wasn't in much pain any more and she felt more optimistic about life. If she was really honest, she was beginning to feel quite proud that she had managed to fend off a serial killer. Her beloved baking had saved the day again. This morning she was still scared to close her eyes and see Savic but after baking she skipped up the stairs feeling as if she could take on the world. Anything that shuts the brain off for a while and gives it the power to reboot is definitely good for the soul. In this case, good food for the soul.

She got undressed in the bedroom and had a last-minute thought before she jumped in the shower. She picked up her phone, opened the camera to face her and placed it on the dressing table. Not quite right. She scoured the room and found two books. She put them on the table and then put the phone on top. "Perfect." She turned on the timer and stepped away. "Three, two, one, snap." She picked up the phone and looked at the picture she had taken of her naked back and bottom. "That should cheer him up," she said to herself. "Forward image to George, message: 'Hurry up and come home xxxx.' Send." She chucked the phone on to the bed and went and began her ablutions. She cast her mind back to the hotel bathroom while scouring Ruth's products. She remembered the marble tiled floor, the golden brass taps, the bath that seemed bottomless. She made a mental note that she and George should book a spa weekend that was a celebration, not about recovery.

Once out and dressed, she skipped downstairs and she could see Ruth sitting on the living room floor with a box of photos.

"What you up to, Mum?"

"Just looking at you when you were a little girl."

"Why?"

"Because I can do what I want." They smiled at each other. Sara picked up a picture of herself. She was topless in a paddling pool.

"I bet in years to come people won't be allowed to take pictures of their own kids like this any more."

"Probably, love. Look at this one. You always did love to look cool."

"That is not a cool look and this photo should be binned before anyone else sees it."

"No way. These are mine."

"Why didn't you tell me how stupid I looked? Look at me. A jumper with shorts, a necklace, dangly earrings and trainers. What was 10-year-old me thinking?"

"Well, when you have your own, you'll love it and you won't want to tell them to get changed. You were expressing yourself. I always loved that about you. The cakes should be cooled now. How about a glass of fizz and some decorating?"

"No. First, hide these photos before anyone else sees them." Sara was jokingly glaring at her mother. "Then cake decorating, followed by fizz and film?"

"OK, dear daughter," Ruth replied obediently.

Ruth said she would ice the carrot cake and that Sara could do her cupcakes. Ruth had a Tupperware box full of dyes and accessories. She always kept it stocked in case Sara wanted to come and bake. She took out the packet of tiny edible icing carrots to decorate her cake, while Sara laid out everything in her arsenal before her. It was concentration time for her. Ruth smoothed the buttercream icing over the top of her perfectly circular sponge and placed tiny carrots all the way around the edge of the cake and she was done. She scooped up a load of the icing with her finger and held it to Sara's mouth.

"Mum, that's gross. Give it to me on a spoon."

"Ten-year-old Sara wouldn't have said that."

"Well, guess what?"

"I know, I know.' Ruth got a teaspoon and piled it high with the icing. "Here you go." Sara slurped it off and licked her lips. They both laughed.

Sara had piped a selection of different coloured icing on to her cupcakes. All 12 of them had been made to look like roses. She chose yellow, orange, pink and white. She had cut out tiny little leaves from green icing and delicately placed them on each perfectly smooth sponge cake. She had sprinkled them with glitter and added edible beads that she had dotted around the icing. They looked straight out of a magazine.

"You should take a picture."

"Of this? Nah."

"Yes. Don't you kids put this stuff on Instagram or something? Go on. I'll bet you get loads of likes."

"OK, if it will keep you happy." She picked up her phone and took a snap, changed the filter and uploaded it with several hashtags about baking.

"It will keep me happy and so do bubbles. I think we deserve a glass, don't you?" Ruth plucked a bottle of chilled prosecco from the fridge while Sara took two flutes from the cupboard.

"What film do you fancy, love?"

"Casablanca, please."

"Here's looking at you, kid." They both smiled and the cork went pop.

The two women took a share-size bag of crisps with their two glasses and settled down in the living room. It started to rain outside and Sara couldn't think of a more perfect setting. She just wanted her beau home with her now.

CHAPTER TWENTY-SEVEN

George was met by a sympathetic team. One of the girls handed him a cup of tea and the biscuit tin as soon as he sat down on the corner of a desk. Mel gave him a hug.

"How are you doing? Silly question, I suppose."

"I just feel overwhelmed, if I'm honest. I've never felt like this before but what with the guv'nor being gone, that was bad enough on its own, you know? I never thought someone would take him down. I always thought he would be here until the bitter end. I've even thought about his retirement party from time to time and imagined how many people would be there and knowing that I would want to pay tribute to him for how he has helped me and my career. I never got to tell him that." George looked down into his hands he had clasped on his lap. "Then there was Sara. I nearly lost her but the mixed bag of emotions that comes with knowing she fought with Savic, that blows my mind. Then there is Christian's son. I mean, none of us saw that coming and you know what, I don't blame him. In my whole career, I've never had to deal with three major incidents so close to me in less than three weeks. I don't know how to be or how to feel. If something makes me laugh I feel guilty and that I shouldn't be able to laugh yet. If I feel sad, my mind tells me to snap out of it. If I close my eyes I see... well, all of it."

Mel put her hand on George's upper arm and smiled at him.

"All you can do is breathe, George. You know that. I would say get some counselling but that is up to you. You are talking now and that's a good thing. You should keep that up with Sara. She needs to talk too. As for the DCI, you were like a son to him. You know he thought the world of you, and as did you him. Look, it's a bit soon but funeral arrangements are being made. Why don't you pay tribute to him there? You could write him a eulogy. I'm sure Pam won't be in any fit state to do it. Visit her and ask the question. We have sent flowers but no one has been to see her yet."

"I don't think I can right now, Mel. That's what I'm saying, if it had just been that, maybe I could've pulled it together but my head still feels like it's underwater at the moment."

"Understandable. Are you ready for your interview now? Best to get it over with, eh?"

George stood up and took his tea and a biscuit into the interview room.

———

Alan had taken himself off to do some errands while George was at the station. He got the car cleaned and took some bottles that had been in the boot to the bottle bank. He then popped into the supermarket for nothing in particular but definitely his weekly lottery ticket. That then led to a wander around the aisles and a trolley loaded with goodies for the weekend. Ruth would raise an eyebrow at the non-cholesterol-friendly purchases but he was one for living. What was meant to be one lottery ticket ended up being a £50 shop.

He was loading the shopping in the car when he got a text from George saying he was ready to be collected now. When Alan pulled up outside the station, an ashen-looking George was waiting there. Alan felt sorry for him and whispered, "The poor lad," under his breath. He could imagine that meeting his girlfriend's parents couldn't have been easy for him but under these circumstances, it must have been awful. He appreciated that he needed room to grieve but he also needed support and Alan didn't feel like he knew him well enough to be of any help.

"All right, lad. It's done now." He looked at him and gave a sympathetic smile. George got in, clipped in his seat belt and sighed. Alan put on Talk Sport and they drove back in silence.

Sara saw the car pull up on the drive and Ruth paused the film. The two men came in and Sara threw her arms around George while Alan and Ruth made themselves scarce.

"How are you, baby?"

"Tired but glad to see you again." He nuzzled into her neck and smelled her hair. "God, I love you. I am so grateful that I don't have to deal with this alone."

"You are never going to have to deal with anything alone for as long as I live."

George squeezed Sara and kissed her on the forehead. They made their way into the kitchen and Alan had poured George a beer. Ruth topped up the prosecco in both glasses and Alan had already been given a slice of carrot cake. There was silence as everyone in the room struggled to find the words to say to anyone.

"Let's go and finish the film, Mum. We're watching Casablanca. Want to watch the rest of it with us?" George was led away by Sara. He was more than happy to sit and do nothing. Sara could see that Dad was happy to sacrifice sport for the next hour and she could see that Mum was about to burst with questions to ask.

The end credits rolled and George started as he realised he had fallen asleep, leaning on Sara. He sat upright and apologised to the room.

"Don't worry, love. You've had a tough day. Do you want to tell us what happened?" Ruth tilted her head and frowned.

"Mum…" Sara said with a warning scowl.

"It's OK." George put his hand on Sara's knee. "I told them everything I could remember but for the first time in my career, I don't remember much. It all happened so fast. It is almost certain that I won't be charged but it's a bitter pill to swallow."

"We understand, love. I told Sara this morning, Alan and I are going out for dinner tonight to give you two some space. We want you to relax."

"Thanks. Honestly, I can't thank you enough." George's mobile began to ring and he furrowed his brow. "It's mum's care home. I haven't been in to see her." The room became tense. George got up from the couch and went into the kitchen to take the call. A few short moments later he returned with a bleak expression.

"They said she hasn't got long and that I should go in to see her."

Sara's heart sank. This was more than even the toughest person could cope with.

"I'll come with you. Let me just grab some things. Dad, are you OK to give us a lift?"

"Of course, honey."

Ruth went into the kitchen and squeezed George's arm as she went past. "I'm so sorry, love."

Sara ran upstairs and hurriedly packed a big handbag, not really knowing what she needed. She put in a deodorant, some make-up, phone charger and some sweets. Her mum knocked gently on the door and let herself in.

"Here. Take this." She handed Sara a bottle of sherry and a new toothbrush.

"What's this for?" Sara was bewildered.

"When my mum, your gran, died, the nurses told me to dip a toothbrush in her favourite drink and rub it on her teeth so it would be the last thing she would taste before she went. I don't know if she was aware of it but I like to think it made it her happy."

"Mum, that is such a lovely idea." Sara packed her mum's offerings into her bag. "How am I going to get him through this, Mum?"

"I don't know, sweetheart, but we will help."

Alan drove Sara and George to the care home. He waved them off with a heavy heart and Sara waved goodbye to him like she did on her very first day of school, not knowing what she was walking into. His little girl really was not a girl any more.

George walked in the front entrance and the look on the staff's faces told him that time was precious. He took in his surroundings, realising that this might be the last time he came here. The tartan couch in the waiting area, the tea and coffee vending machine, the slightly odd smell of old people mixed with cleaning products.

They were led to the room which was half way down the corridor. Some of the residents were sitting in the communal area and some were getting about with their walking frames. The nurse opened the door to room of George's mother, Gladys. The television was on quietly and the bedside lamp was lit. She had a trolley tray across her with non-spill cups containing various different liquids. On the side was an unopened box of shortbread. Sara looked around at the photos on the walls of George and other family members she hadn't yet met. Someone clearly had a child as there was a youngster's paintings on the walls.

Sara then looked at George's mum. She was lying on her back. Her skin was already looking grey and her mouth was wide open. Her eyes were closed but would very nearly open occasionally. A gentle flicker of recognition. She knew someone was with her. George sat on the edge of the bed. Sara stood next to him and placed her arm on his shoulders.

"I can't believe I didn't come in to see her. It should have been the first thing I did when I got out."

Sara felt a pang of guilt. George took his mother's frail hand in both of his and brought it to his mouth. He kissed her gently and placed it back flat along her side.

"I love you mum. I'll miss you so much. I owe you everything. Thank you for making me the man I am today." His nose started to stream and he lowered his head, wiping away tears. Sara felt a lump rise in her throat and wished she could take this man's the pain away.

Sara and George sat silently for a while and just watched Gladys breathing. The silence was soothing for them after what had been a chaotic time. Although George was sombre, he was prepared for what was coming.

"This kind of brings back memories of Rachel. My wife."

"We haven't spoken about her yet. Why don't you tell me now?"

"Rachel worked in the force too. We met at work. Almost eight years ago now since we met. We got together and had a happy relationship. We never had a cross word. Not once. It was easy. We holidayed together, went out for dinners, weekends away, concerts. It was just a normal relationship that worked. We got married. I wanted kids but she said she wanted to wait. She wanted to focus on her career for a while. I had no issue with that. Then one night when she was out working, I got a call. There had been a car crash. I went to the hospital and got to say goodbye but she was unconscious. She died 27 minutes later. Then, before I could get over the shock, it became clear she had not been working. She had been having an affair with a colleague. They had been found together in her car which was pulled over into a lay-by on a fast A-road. A lorry driver had a heart attack at the wheel and ploughed into the car. They both died. Him instantly. The lorry driver survived but was traumatised. Her colleagues confirmed she wasn't on shift that night and I knew straight away. I don't know why I hadn't seen it before then but think I must have been in some sort of denial. I knew she had been cheating on me. The guy's wife didn't want to believe it. We don't speak now. I don't know what she is up to these days. Anyway, I put on a brave face for the funeral and then I took all of her possessions to her sister's. I told her I needed to cut the cord with them all and didn't want to stay in touch and I never have. It was better for me that way. So, that was Rachel. My first wife, killed in a car accident while having an affair."

"Oh George. You really do deserve a break. I can't promise to make you happy every day but I will never break your heart."

"I think you will make me happy every day. Just by being mine."

They cuddled tightly smelling each other's shoulders and feeling like home together. Sara got up to go and get some tea and promised to be back in a minute. George looked at Gladys. He was so sad to be watching his mother's last moments but was glad to have found Sara. He knew she was a better match for him than Rachel ever was. Sara came back into the room balancing two cups of tea on saucers.

"George, I have an idea. Does your mum like sherry?"

"Yeah she's always loved the stuff." He rubbed away some tears and sniffed loudly.

"Here. Dip this toothbrush in this sherry and rub it along her teeth. She might be able to enjoy the taste before she goes."

George looked at Sara and smiled.

"You're such a sweet girl."

Sara shrugged. She handed him the toothbrush and the bottle and let him do what she had suggested. She saw a card on the bedside table addressed to Gladys. So that was her name.

"Gladys, I am going to take good care of your son. You don't need to worry. He is going to be loved so much and thank you for raising him so well. He really is the man of my dreams."

Gladys blinked and they both saw it. It was the last time she did. A while later, Sara went and got a member of staff who confirmed that she had gone. The doctor came in and offered George a moment longer with his mum. Sara quietly popped out of the room to call her parents.

A few slow and sad hours later, George and Sara were back at her parent's house. Everything that could be done today had been done. The care home would keep him informed as to what had to be done next. Gladys had been taken to the morgue. There was nothing else that could be done this evening.

Ruth and Alan decided to stay in and Ruth had made her signature beef Wellington. Sara took George upstairs so they could have a lie-down together. The pair of them lay side by side, holding hands and staring at the ceiling.

"It doesn't matter how prepared you are, you're never really prepared, are you?" George was still sniffling but trying to hold it back.

"Nope. How can you ever be prepared for something like that? Where do they go? That's the big thing for most people, I think. How can a whole life, a whole person who lived that long, brought you into the world, had a job, had a marriage, had likes and dislikes, had 80 years' worth of memories and experiences just suddenly be gone like a light that's gone out? We all leave a footprint on this earth but not everyone gets to see it."

George rolled over and snuggled into Sara.

"I'll be OK tomorrow. I just need to get tonight out of the way."

"Don't you dare rush it. Take as long as you need and keep talking to me. I think bottling things up leads to a much worse grieving period."

"You are such a sweet girl. I came into your life wanting to protect you and look after you. I never knew I would need you so much."

"I'm beginning to think that's why we were brought together. Most people have the most fun at the beginning of a new romance and then the problems and disappointment set in. Our love story wasn't meant to be one of fireworks and romance and laughter and fun, not at first. Our romance is about needing and supporting and genuine care. We are getting to start with what most people aspire to. We will get our fun later, built on the solid foundation of a tremendous love for each other. In a weird way, maybe we are lucky."

"I know I am lucky. I feel like everything has led me to you. It has all been worth it."

"I love you, George Ramsay. Let's go and have some of Mum's dinner, otherwise *she* won't love you."

CHAPTER TWENTY-EIGHT

Three weeks had passed and George had buried his beloved mother. Although she was in her eighties, it was a fairly large gathering because of all the family she had left behind her. It was a strange setting but Sara got to meet George's aunts, uncles and his cousins. She also met his brother, his brother's wife and their young son who had flown in from Vancouver. The young son was responsible for all the artwork in Gladys's room. He was six years old and his name was Ethan. George's brother, Nick, was a comic book artist and very cool. Their whole family unit was cool. Sara warmed to them as they did to her. Ethan in particular bonded with her very quickly, which made her happy on such a sombre day.

It was a moving service and George read a beautiful eulogy to his mother. It was clear that he had idolised her. Now that she had met his brother Nick, she could see that they were related but they were very different men. Nick looked and came across as though he belonged in a sophisticated big city like Vancouver and George was very British with a strong sense of justice and old-fashioned traits.

George had invited Ruth and Alan to the funeral, too. It made sense to him. He had already decided that the families were intertwined now. He also wanted Sara to have some support there as he knew he would be busy talking to everyone who attended. Ruth in particular appreciated the gesture. After the long and arduous day, they all went back to Ruth and Alan's. Sara and George, drained from it all, went to bed early. George slept holding Sara until morning.

It was a Wednesday afternoon and the two of them were sitting in the living room watching a Christmas film. To Sara's surprise, George had chosen an animation. He was a big kid at heart. She saw him as a black and white movie kind of guy, serious and moody but with an uplifting ending.

"I don't want to go back to work yet. I have been so happy, strangely, getting through this awful time with you," George murmured, stroking Sara's fingers.

"If I'm honest, I don't want to go back, either. I want to spend every minute with you, but –and there is a but – we have a new house to move into soon and that won't pay for itself. Sadly, you and I will be working for many more years to come yet."

"True. Fancy going on holiday?"

"When?"

"Tomorrow."

"Tomorrow? Sara echoed.

"Yeah. We could go to Paris for a weekend. Treat ourselves."

"No. I can't."

"Why?"

"Oh, you'll laugh at me if I tell you. OK, I just have this thing. I've always wanted to go there. In fact, it is my dream to go there but I only want to go there for one thing. It's one of the most romantic cities in the world and so, you know, that's where I want to get engaged." Sara blushed at looked down at her lap. "I also wanted it be a surprise and now it won't be because if you ever tell me we are going to Paris, I will know why."

George looked deep in thought and Sara was willing him to hurry up and break the awkward silence she had created.

"Sounds like you are going to have to come up with a new idea then because I would want it to be a surprise too. Why don't you come up with another dream? Then we can go to Paris tomorrow anyway."

George could pretty much see the cogs turning in Sara's head.

"Come on. We would be in a hotel on our own. We haven't had our own space for ages. We could try and put the last few horrible weeks out of mind and just do some Christmas shopping while indulging in wine and amazing food. Don't tell your mum I said that. You do love staying in hotels, I know that much. Come on."

Sara's phone started ringing.

"It's an unknown number. Great. I had better go and take it. I'll think about Paris." She called behind her as she left the room.

When Sara returned, she opened the living room door to find George kneeling on one knee with a little velvet box in his hand. He had turned the television off and lit several tea lights and placed them along the mantelpiece. The lights on the Christmas tree were on and the curtains were closed. The fire was already burning. She stopped in her tracks completely unprepared for what she had walked into.

"George."

"What if you were already engaged the first time you went to Paris?'

Sara brought her hand to her mouth and gasped. She was

frozen to the spot. He shuffled forward on one knee until he was by her foot.

"So, Sara Edgerton. Would you make me the happiest man alive and be my wife?" Sara said nothing. She looked at him and then at the ring and then back at him. "We don't need to get married. I know it's only been a few months but I know I want you for ever. What we have been through has brought us together. Now I want us to look after each other for the rest of our lives. I never want you to face anything alone. I want to be the one who you come home to after a rubbish day. You can tell me about your colleagues that you don't like and I will pour you a glass of wine. You can complain that you are so tired because you have been up with the baby all night and I will run you a bath and tell you I will do it tonight. You will come home and there will be a bottle of your favourite perfume on the table with some flowers from time to time, just because. Then there will be all the mornings we get to have breakfast together. Sometimes in bed and sometimes in the garden. We can both work on our doing-up-the-house project. We can learn gardening together. We can build an extension one year that will cause many arguments but it will be worth it because we will fall in to bed together every night. I want you for every sickness and cold and bug you get. I want you for every moment that makes you happy and share it with you. I will watch any of your girly films that you want to watch. I would even buy your tampons if you sent me out to get them. I'd learn Spanish for you if you decide you want to retire abroad. I want you for everything that you are and more."

"Yes, George, yes."

She flung her arms around him and they kissed. Not for long, though. Sara wanted to see the ring and try it on. It was stunning. An emerald cut diamond set in a platinum band.

"George, it's perfect. I can't believe it. I don't know what to say."

"You've said everything I needed to hear tonight. I couldn't propose in Paris like I wanted to, little Miss Impatient Pants, but I could deliver a surprise. I hope you are not disappointed."

"Disappointed? How on earth could I be disappointed? Just look at you. You are really mine? For as long as we both live." She cuddled him.

"Always and for ever and even beyond that."

There was a knock at the door.

"Can we come in now?" Ruth and Alan walked in, Ruth clutching a bottle of champagne.

"You knew?" Sara asked, beaming.

"Well yes but we also knew he wouldn't be able to propose in Paris once he told you that's where he was taking you so we jumped the gun and bought a bottle. Let's get some glasses."

The family toasted George and Sara's engagement. George was still struggling to process how much he had lost and gained in the last few months. He kept looking at Sara's big smile and how she kept looking at her ring and, even though he felt like he had been through so much, he now felt like his life was just beginning.

"Guys, there is something else I need to tell you, too," Sara announced.

Ruth, Alan and George looked at each other in bewilderment.

"You're not..? Ruth gestured to her tummy.

"Oh Mum, again? No,I am not. No, you remember how you told me to post that picture of my cakes on Instagram? Well, a company called me just a moment ago and want to meet me. They saw my picture and they said they thought I was a food photographer. They want me to go out and have an interview."

"Go out and have an interview?" Ruth looked panic-stricken.

"Yes. Their headquarters are in San Francisco. George, they said we can both go out for five days, all expenses paid."

"You won't move there, will you?" Ruth seemed to be on the verge of losing it.

"No. They said some travel will be involved to their offices in London, New York, San Francisco and Hong Kong but that it's a mainly work-from-home position. They are looking for a UK-based representative and they want to talk to me."

The room was silent while everyone waited to see George's reaction.

"Honey that is amazing. Let's go for it. I will be behind you every step of the way."

Everyone in the room toasted again and Alan got out another bottle of champagne.

"I've got to say, kids, it's been a weird one. I wouldn't normally be happy about my daughter getting engaged so soon but I am genuinely thrilled for you both. You've been through hell and you're coming out the other side. You have my blessing without a doubt."

Sara gave her dad a hug.

"You're my first hero, always, Dad. George, they want us to go to San Francisco on Monday. Can we do Paris when we get back?"

"Of course we can. I can delay the hotel and the flights weren't expensive. This is more important."

'It's snowing! It's snowing!' Ruth shrieked. She came into the living room and opened the curtains. Sara looked out and George hugged her from behind. The two of them watched in silence as the snowflakes fell. George squeezed Sara and she rested her head on him. Ruth and Alan looked at each other and smiled. Alan put his arm around Ruth to her surprise and they cuddled and then joined George and Sara and they all took a moment to watch the snow fall under the light of the street lamps outside.

CHAPTER TWENTY-NINE

George and Sara checked in for their flight at London Heathrow. Ruth and Alan were there waving them off, even though Sara had told them there was no need for them to come. They both looked behind them before heading to security. They stopped and waved enthusiastically at Sara's parents who were beaming as if she had just come on stage in her first nativity play.

Once through security, George and Sara walked hand in hand and felt the furthest away from their troubles that they had done since it all started. They were free to be out and stroll along or sit in a restaurant or a bar and not have to look over their shoulders. If there was one place they were safe it was in an airport. Sara pondered how they were completely safe now. Christian was behind bars as was Savic. Christian's son's attack was shocking but it was unlikely that the younger one would follow suit. They were free now. Sara squeezed George's hand at that thought. He looked at her as she smiled up at him and he smiled back down to her.

"How do you fancy going to the champagne and oyster bar?" George was striding through the airport with the air of confidence he'd had when they first met.

"Champagne yes, oysters at this time of day I'm not sure. To be honest, I'd be happy having a glass of prosecco at Wetherspoons with a bacon roll."

"I know you would and I like that but we are celebrating. Celebrating many things so let me buy us some champagne. We deserve it. You deserve it."

Sara felt giddy on love and that was before she had even had the bubbles. They pulled up two bar stools and the barman greeted them immediately. Sara nudged George. "Do you always get better service when paying through the nose?" she asked.

"Oh yeah. Very rarely worth it but it's worth every penny this time. We'll have a bottle of this one please." George pointed to one on the list and handed it back to the barman.

"Very nice choice, sir." The barman nodded and presented them with a plate of seafood. George declined the offer and raised his glass in a toast.

"To my girl. The fighter, the tough cookie and my fiancée."

They clinked glasses and kissed.

"We deserve this, don't we? I mean, how quickly everything has changed – and there is no one else I would rather spend it with than you."

They sat at the bar for an hour while they waited for their flight to be called. They watched all the busy travellers rushing past, some on business, some going on holiday, some coming home, some perhaps going to see someone for the last time. Couples in the shops, lone travellers drinking coffee, important people in suits having important conversations on their mobiles. The overworked plugging their laptops in on the communal worktops doing that last bit of work before they had to log off. Children running around, their excitement getting them into trouble. Siblings squabbling. Hen parties giggling. *Airports are a world of their own,* Sara thought.

George and Sara washed down the rest of their bubbles and George picked up the bill.

"Come on. One more thing before we board." He took Sara's hand and guided her into one of the exclusive luggage outlets. "I think you should go to this meeting of yours with a fancy satchel," he told her.

Sara opened her mouth to object but George hushed her with a finger against her lips. "If you don't pick one, then I will just pick one for you."

"Pick one for me anyway. This is a gift from you and I trust your style. You choose."

George scoured his eyes along the bag collection and picked out a tan leather one with a subtle little bow on it. Sara had her arm linked in his, the whole time. They went to the till and in the blink of an eye it was bought with George's card and it was being wrapped in tissue paper. The cash assistant pulled out a fancy cardboard bag from under the till and Sara thought it was almost as pretty as the one that George had just paid hundreds of pounds for. As they walked out, Sara was pecking George's cheek repeatedly.

Leaving, the shop, Sara reflected that she had a treat in each hand. A brand new satchel in one and her lover in the other. Their flight was called and they happily made their way to the gate. Sara joined the end of the queue and George looked at her, puzzled.

"What are you doing?"

"Queuing," Sara replied.

"Sara, the tickets they bought us are business class. We don't queue."

Sara's face lit up. "Ooh. That's new." They made their way to the desk and Sara thought the check-in clerk seemed friendlier than her colleague on the economy desk. Sara wondered if that was part of the service, too. As they made their way along the tunnel to their plane, Sara said: "I don't really see the point in jumping the queue. We aren't going anywhere until everyone is on the plane."

"Give it a minute. You'll see."

Sara looked puzzled and made her way on to the aircraft.

"Champagne madam?" The flight attendant had taken her carry-on case and was helping her out of her coat from her to hang it in the locker.

Sara beamed as she looked back at George. "OK, now I get it."

George winked at her and Sara thought this was turning out to be the best week of her life.

They were shown to their seats and Sara was like a small child in a sweet shop for the first time. She looked over the menu in amazement.

"You can have afternoon tea in business class. You can have a choice of champagnes in business class." She gazed at George in disbelief. He was chuckling to himself. She put the menu down and got into her seat. "I have my own bed. And look at this washbag. Leather. I never want to fly in economy ever again."

"Better hope this job pays well, then, or we won't be having many holidays."

They clinked their small glasses of champagne.

"And glass? You don't get glass in economy."

"Take it all in, girl. Enjoy every minute. You deserve it."

Their stewardess came over and gave them two new glasses of champagne and asked them if they needed anything else and if that if they did they could buzz at any time, it would be no trouble at all.

A short while later, the cabin lights were dimmed and they were preparing for take-off. George and Sara were going to San Francisco.

CHAPTER THIRTY

George opened the door to their hotel room and Sara walked in before him. She dropped her bags on the floor and gasped. George was smiling behind her, for her.

"You did say you wanted another hotel stay soon. Ask and you shall receive, apparently." Sara rushed forward to the blinds, struggling to open them. "Honey, here."

George passed her a remote that seemed to control everything in the room. The curtains began to pull back in front of them and they both looked out over the high-rises of the city.

"Wow. Wow, wow, wow." She was now grinning at George like a Cheshire cat. "Are we really here? Are we really here, George?"

He stood behind her and put his arms around her. Kissing her softly on the head, he said: "We sure are."

Sara pulled away and looked around the room, continuing to smile as if it was Christmas Day about 20 years ago. She hopped about, opening doors, pirouetting like a ballerina.

"There are two bathrooms, George." She called. "This hotel room is epic."

"It's a suite, honey. Whoever this company are, they are pretty serious about you. Now let's decide what you want to do tonight."

"Wow, I've never stayed in a suite before. How much do you reckon this cost? I don't think we should go wild tonight. Big meeting tomorrow and all that."

"OK, great. We can ask the concierge for some restaurant recommendations. But first, give me a kiss. And close the curtains while you're up."

Sara looked around at George, who was smiling suggestively at her.

Walking towards him, she crawled on to the bed and hovered above him. Gently she kissed him on the mouth.

"We don't need to close the curtains in a room like this."

George looked like he was about to explode. He growled at her and pulled her closer.

A post-coital shower and a fancy coffee each later, George and Sara were ready to explore their surroundings. Sara was sitting at the desk putting on the keepers of her earrings.

"I bloody love holidays. What is it about them that makes everything better. Sex on holiday is better."

"Whoa there, steady."

"Oh, but come on, it is. It's the excitement. Even the coffee is more exciting. Look at that machine. That probably cost more than all of my crockery put together."

"Do you not like our sex at home?"

Sara jumped up and gave him a squeeze.

"I love sex with you anywhere. It has never been bad. Better? Come on, let's go." Without waiting, she made her way out of the room while George quickly scanned the room for his essentials. He had his wallet and his phone. That was all he needed. The door closed behind him and Sara was already standing by the lifts.

"Do you think any celebrities have stayed here?"

"Probably. It's a pretty nice hotel."

"Wow. I could be walking on the same carpet as Britney. Do you really think Britney might have stayed here?"

"Not sure, babe. Maybe. Just go with maybe. I've looked on TripAdvisor and there seem to be some pretty cool bars and places to eat nearby so I suggest we just go for a stroll and see what takes your fancy."

The doors to the lift opened.

"I've already had what I fancied today."

As the doors opened, George and Sara were met with a disapproving-looking older couple. Sara gave a toothy grin to her visibly embarrassed beau.

Sara was wrapped up in a little woollen hat, a chunky knitted scarf and fleece-lined mittens. George's bright red ears said that they wished he was wearing a hat. The pair strolled around the streets aimlessly along street after street of high-rises, often with knots of people huddled together, smoking. After a short while, they stopped at an Italian restaurant they found on a side street. Sara peered through the window and could see between the gap of the frilly window lining and the menu taped up that there were people sitting at the bar as well as a couple of tables of diners.

"Let's go in here. It would be nice to have a glass of warming red in this weather."

They walked in and pulled out two bar stools. George nodded to the barman.

"Two glasses of merlot, please." He gave Sara's cheek a slow stroke. "I'm glad to be out of that weed smoke. I can't believe they have legalised that here. Not a good idea, if you ask me."

"You know what would be a good idea? Us finding you a

hat and gloves before this day is over." George rolled his eyes and they clinked glasses. "I still can't believe we are here, George."

Images of Christian, Savic and blood spatter started to fill Sara's mind. Goosebumps raised on her arms. Hospital, pushing George away and then going to his hotel with him. That first night when they patched things up. Her eyes dilated. George meeting her parents. She was feeling warm now. Christian's son attacking them. A cold shiver ran over her. She shook her head and wanted the images to fall out like little polaroids from her ears as she did so.

George was watching Sara and trying to get her attention. He knew exactly what she was thinking and when she was thinking it. With each different facial expression or twitch, he relived it with her.

"Sara? Sara?"

"Sorry." She was back in the room now.

"Don't think, honey. This trip is about your talent and success. Don't let anyone or anything cloud that for you."

They drank their red wine. In between sips they would hold hands. One minute tightly and then loosely with George stroking Sara's little hand with his thumb. They decided to have another. They were relaxed now and enjoying listening to the cacophony of San Francisco accents, the harassed staff, the subtle restaurant music and they even liked being asked if they were from London by each waiter who spoke to them. Sara would tell them they were from the south coast of England but the waiters' eyes would glaze over and George would say it was near London and they would be all smiles again. Most of them knew someone in London and would enthusiastically tell them all about it.

They left the bar in a fog of merlot and jet lag. All the shops had closed and so they giggled their way across to a

Target to buy George a hat and some gloves. He tried on some children's ones and referred to Sara as his mum. She promised not to nag him too much in their lives together but said she wouldn't take no for an answer on this one. She said in exchange for her bullying she would take him for a burger and a beer and then she would be ready for bed. George agreed and they found a nice little bar on Grove Street.

Sara went to freshen up once they ordered food. George took out his phone and looked at his emails. He froze when he saw what had come in from work. He read it and reread it but still couldn't get his head around what he was reading. He put his phone face down and rubbed his forehead. The screech of Sara's chair on the flag stone tiles alerted him.

"This place is great. It seems really American, you know? Very authentic."

George smiled, took her hand and brought it to his mouth and gave it a soft kiss. "You're such a softy. Don't change."

Sara looked at him askance. "

"What's up?"

George batted off her suspicion with a confused look.

"Nothing. Why?"

"You seem different. Something is bothering you. What is it?"

"Nothing. Honestly, just feeling a bit tired."

Sara knew that look and she'd heard that lie before. She was desperate to push for the truth but decided to leave it and see how he was in the morning. *Perhaps I'm just tired, too,* she thought.

———

The sound of Sara's phone alarm woke them abruptly. They hadn't had to set an alarm since that fateful night. George rolled over and pushed his face into the pillow and pulled the duvet up over his head. Sara sat up immediately and stretched her arms out wide above her head. She picked up the remote and told the blinds to open, still smiling at how cool that was. Her eyes widened as the San Francisco skyline began to fill the vast window. If she didn't have the interview of her life today, she could sit and stare at that view for hours. She got out of bed, causing minimal disruption to George who was twitching in a way that said he was losing his battle with going back to sleep. The luxurious carpet oozed luxuriously between her toes as she walked to the bathroom. She felt as if she were looking at the room again for the first time as they had been so jaded when they arrived yesterday. Cream walls, mahogany furniture, a royal blue chesterfield sofa. The carpet was a shade off champagne and felt three times as thick as any carpet she had ever stood on. The suite was large, bigger than some flats in London, she thought. The windows were floor-to-ceiling and looked out over the financial district in the city. She ran her finger along the dresser as she made her way to the bathroom. She wanted to soak up every bit of this room because this could be one of those moments in life she only lived once. The bathroom had a walk-in shower with the option of a rainforest shower head or a detachable shower head. She had never seen one like that before. There was a bath on the other side of the room – she would explore that later. She turned on the rainforest shower and the water plummeted down like a waterfall and quickly the room began to steam. She left the door open so she could see the view at all times. She never wanted not to see that skyline.

George and Sara left the hotel, hand in hand and with a spring in their step. A good night's sleep, aided with a melatonin tablet each and they were feeling brand new. They had discussed the interview only briefly. George hadn't wanted to keep on in case she was nervous. She seemed excited, despite confessing that she didn't really know what was expected of her.

The cab took them to a very shiny skyscraper. Sara really had to crane her neck to see up to the top of it. They smiled at each other and made their way into the building. The receptionist was seriously funky. She had electric-blue hair that had been styled into a high ponytail with a victory roll on top. She was wearing a black leather waistcoat with nothing underneath. Her arms were tattooed from top to bottom and Sara found herself looking at a naked woman draped over a motorbike on her forearm. Her bottom lip had a hoop through the centre along with a hoop through her right nostril and one through her left eyebrow. Her lips were painted raspberry pink and her eyebrows looked tattooed on. Sara thought she looked incredible. She looked down at herself. Skinny jeans, pumps and a floral blouse with a mustard yellow cashmere coat. *How bloody British,* she thought to herself, thinking the receptionist would think she looked daggy.

"I love your coat. That colour is sick," said the receptionist, whose name tag showed she was called Evangeline.

Sara blushed. Evangeline thought she was cool. She tried to say thanks back but no words came out. Evangeline smiled, pointed to the seats and said she would bring them some water.

George was walking round the walls. There were a few magazine covers dotted around in frames with very famous people adorning them.

"So, this is Bulletin headquarters." Sara picked up a magazine and flicked through it. Before George could answer, Evangeline said they were ready for her. Sara looked at George and gulped. He winked at her and her stomach flipped. It got her every time. She smiled at him and stood up straight.

Shoulders back, she ordered herself. Whatever this was about, she was going to give it her best shot.

Evangeline opened the door to a studio. There were three people on the panel sitting at the back of the room. The other three walls were white. In the middle was a table with various items on it and a camera.

"Sara Edgerton. Thank you for coming to see us," Said a woman with a jet-black crisp bob and porcelain skin.

"No. Thank *you*," She replied enthusiastically.

"Oh God, I love her accent." That was said by a hipster. He had circular glasses on that took up most of his face and what looked like drawn-on freckles.

"Sara, we won't take up much of your time. We are all busy. On the table are some items. We want you to photograph them in whatever way you want. Show us some pizzazz. We are bored and looking for panache." The third panel member had spoken. Now all she had to do was deliver.

Sara looked at the table of props. A plate of cupcakes not unlike the ones she had made. A selection of vintage books. A bowl of old mobile phones. A selection of travel photographs. Some make-up. Coins. A deck of playing cards.

She stared at what was in front of her and closed her eyes. *Think Sara, think.* She looked in her handbag and was relieved to see she had packed some wipes. She set out the travel photos in a messy yet organised way. She picked up the coins and climbed up on top of the table, which caught razor-bob's attention. Hovering over the photos, she gently released the coins over them. She hopped back down and looked inside her bag and found a train ticket and a leaflet map of the city. She screwed the train ticket up in her hand and tossed it on to the table. She held the map in her hand and looked at various angles as to where it should go. She decided on the bottom left hand corner. Then she got a pink lipstick from the props and drew a love heart in the top right-hand corner. Once again, she climbed up on the table and took a picture from up above. She could see the panel whispering, just a few feet away from her but paid them no attention. She took several shots and cleared the counter using her wipes to clean up the lipstick.

Next, she picked up the cakes and had begun to arrange them when she had an idea. She took them over to the panel and placed a cupcake on the drawn-on-freckles-guy's head. She told him to look up to his left and stick a tiny bit of his tongue out. He did and she snapped away. Now it was razor-bob's turn. She asked her to take a big bite out of the cake so it would be half-in and half-out, while looking directly at her. Razor-bob paused and number three told her to get on with it. Razor-bob did as she was told. Snap. Number three looked in bewilderment as Sara stared at him. She leaned forward and squashed a cupcake perfectly on his nose and positioned it so it stayed in place. Razor bob looked like she was about to explode. Snap. Sara took the cake off and gave him a wipe.

Following that, she did a final display back on the table and was told she had done enough. Circle glasses looked impressed but as for razor bob and number three, she couldn't tell. She smiled at them, shook their hands and said goodbye. She had done what she could.

That afternoon George and Sara took a cab to Sausalito – of course they had to go over the Golden Gate Bridge while they were there. They headed to a burger bar that was hotly tipped online as the best in the town. Sara regaled George with what happened at the interview. They both laughed as she told him she didn't have a "hope in hell" of getting the job so decided to have some fun with it. After all, "When are we likely to be back in San Francisco again?"

The burgers did not disappoint, despite nearly being bigger than Sara's head. A soft brioche bun not nearly enough to hold together the 2lb burger with oozing Monterey Jack cheese dripping out of the sides, giving the gherkins and tomatoes something to cling on to. The lettuce was in there just to make up the numbers. After Sara had tried and failed to eat it like a lady, George told her to get stuck in and surrender to the mess.

Sara noticed George's phone going off several times. At first, she thought he was ignoring it because he was eating but, even after then, when they were having a beer, he seemed to have messages coming in and not looking at them. He saw her looking and turned his phone over face down on the table. Sara recalled feeling anxious last night before they went to bed. He was hiding something and, last time he did that, it was not good. Her anxiety was now kicking back in.

"George, why aren't you looking at your phone?"

"Oh, it's just work. I'll speak to them later."

"You aren't hiding something from me again, are you?"

"Can we talk about this later? I want this trip to be about you."

Sara's fears were not allayed. She wanted to know right away what the problem was. How could she possibly relax now? It was something bad. It had to be for him to behave this way. Savic had escaped? Christian had escaped? Christian was being released? It couldn't be that, he had been charged and was awaiting trial. The trial. Maybe it was the trial date. But then, she would be notified of that too.

"Honey, please relax. It's nothing to worry about."

"Well, what is it? I can't relax now. I'm not going to stop coming up with scenarios in my head until you put my mind at ease."

George put his beer down and cleared his throat. "OK. It is work. They want me to replace DCI Wilson. They want to make me Chief Inspector."

Sara almost knocked the table over as she lurched forward to hug him.

"George, that's amazing. It's what you always wanted. It's what you have been working towards. Why would you keep that from me? This is a double celebration now."

George smiled tightly. "I don't know, Sara. It seems tainted now. I didn't want it under these circumstances. I didn't want the boss dead, you know."

Sara placed her hands over his and smiled sympathetically.

"No one wanted that but I bet DCI Wilson wouldn't want anyone else stepping in to take over his good work. You are the man for the job. It's what he would have wanted.'

"And what about this? What if you get this job.?"

"Don't be daft, George. I won't get the job."

But George had a feeling she might.

CHAPTER THIRTY-ONE

George and Sara spent the last couple of days taking in everything San Francisco had to offer. They visited Alcatraz, walking hand in hand and listening to the history of the inmates on their headsets. They went to Pier 39 for fresh crab and laughed at the plastic tuxedo-style bibs they were given to wear. They scaled Lombard Street, the infamous steep road with eight hairpin turns. George was fit enough to make it look easy but Sara had to pretend it wasn't a struggle.

They ate delicious food and had their fair share of alcohol but now it was time to pack up and leave. Sara took her time, knowing she would likely never stay in a hotel like this one again. She thought to herself how nice it would be to live in this kind of luxury as she picked up the vanity kit and miniatures from the bathroom. When she came out, George had gone. Sara delicately began folding her clothes and packing them away, taking more time than usual because she didn't want this to end. When they got back to England, there would be the trial and they would be living with her parents again. This trip had been the perfect escape for them. At times, she hadn't even thought much at all about what had happened but now that she was packing to go home, she couldn't think of anything else.

———

The airliner touched down on its runway at Heathrow with a gentle thud. Rain splattered against the small windows. Sara sighed as she looked out at the grey outdoors. It was Christmas eve and there was not a fleck of snow in sight. This wasn't going to be white Christmas, it was going to be an "all right" Christmas. She was struggling to see the positives, even though she knew they were there. They seemed out of reach and her heart lay heavy in the pit of her stomach. The whirlwind trip to San Francisco was over and the murder trial was knocking at the door. Sara was overwhelmed at the prospect of having to relive the ordeal that had been Hallowe'en. She had a physical ache at the idea of seeing Christian again. She had hoped the plane would never land and that they would just fly and fly and never have to face up to reality.

George took Sara's hand and gave it a squeeze. She knew she was being too quiet but she didn't think she could talk to him about how she was feeling. He wouldn't want to hear that she was thinking about Christian. She couldn't tell him at all. She gave him a half-hearted smile and prised herself out of her seat. Every step she took was a step closer to facing their next hurdle and she didn't want to do it. As she trudged forward reluctantly, she wondered what everyone else was facing. *Most of the passengers on this flight must be going to be with their families*, she thought. *They are heading into holiday season bliss. Woolly jumpers, succulent turkey, mounds of veg and mulled wine. Laughing and exchanging gifts.* She could picture it clearly. *But not me. I have a murder trial hanging over me.*

Before they knew it, they were home and Sara was

surprised to find that it actually did lift her spirits. There was something about safety in numbers. Having Mum and Dad around offered plenty of distraction and walking in to the smell of freshly cooked cottage pie awoke Sara's senses and offered her great comfort. Sure, the food in San Francisco was to die for but nothing could beat Ruth's cottage pie.

George watched Sara and Ruth go through all their pictures from their trip. He could tell she was being distant and he didn't know how to help. He wanted to give her time to approach him but also felt as though he could do with some attention himself. He was nervous about spending Christmas Day with his sudden new family. Although they had been so kind and generous with their home, he still felt a little bit out of place. He would just have to ride this one out and then they could all come to his and Sara's place next year.

———

Sara woke up to the sound of Cliff Richard playing downstairs. She rubbed her eyes and rolled over to cuddle George.

"It's Christmas," she whispered in his ear. He pulled her on to him and they shared a long, warm embrace. "Ready for Christmas at the Edgertons'?"

"Ready as I'll ever be."

The day was exactly what George and Sara needed. The house was full of aunts and uncles, cousins and granny. Ruth had her Christmas album on repeat and the table was laid to Christmas perfection. Ruth's table centrepiece, always the talk of any family event, was a marvel of holly, acorns, ribbons and fake snow. The food was never-ending and there seemed to be course after course. Sara was given the job of going around with the plates of entrées. Ruth had made little tiny vol-au-vent's, chicken and pepper skewers, the inevitable cheese and pineapple sticks and some mini savoury eggs. Cooking was her theatre and she loved nothing more than to flaunt her culinary prowess to the family. It was when she was at her happiest, feeding the people she loved.

Gifts were exchanged and George was now fully stocked with new socks and bathroom kits. Sara was equally well stocked with bathroom kits and slippers. They gave each other only a couple of small gifts because they were saving every spare penny for the new house. That had been the plan but, after George's proposal, Sara felt he should have an engagement gift, too. She had picked out an expensive watch while they had been away and sent the link to Ruth to collect it and have it engraved with the day they met.

By the evening, the family were done in. The relatives had left, the cleaning up had been finished and the four of them, almost ready to pop with all of the food they had eaten, collapsed in front of the television to watch a Christmas film. Sara held her hand out and looked at her ring glistening. She smiled at George who looked at his new watch and then her, smiling sheepishly.

Sara didn't know why she had been so worried about coming home. Their first Christmas together had been perfect. Having all of her family around her had been like paracetamol for her fears. The things that had worried her didn't even get thought about. She realised that the best thing was to keep busy and keep going.

George didn't know why he had been worried about spending Christmas with Sara's family. Everyone was keen to meet him and ask lots of questions and one of her aunties in particular was definitely a big fan of George, which they both found amusing. He had been warned about Beryl. She had been widowed for almost 20 years and was clearly missing having a man in her life. They all made him feel so welcome and it didn't seem for one minute as if he had been around for only three months. He knew Sara and he had a tough hurdle ahead of them but he felt more secure now than ever and knew that, oddly, it would bring them closer together.

———

It was three months later and George and Sara were standing on the steps outside the crown court. They held each other as Sara sobbed heavily on George's shoulder. She was shaking uncontrollably. It was over. It was done and all they had now was a future ahead of them where they could plan their happiness together.

Christian had been sentenced to life, with the condition that he would have to serve 22 years before being considered for parole. His barrister tried to claim that he had helped the police after his arrest but it was a weak defence. The judge and the jury saw right through it. Savic was also handed a life sentence but, in his case, it was a minimum term of 40 years, meaning that he would probably die in prison. He had nothing to say. He refused to comment, shrugged and accepted his fate.

George was a free but changed man. He read out a statement to the salivating press. He told them about the sentencing, the horror for everyone involved, that justice had been done and that the scars and memories would fade. Sara held his hand but kept her head down. Their faces would be all over the news. The case was huge. A jealous jilted lover hires a hitman and ends up killing his own wife. It was incomprehensible for most people but it was very real to Sara, George and the surviving members of Christian's family.

———

Susan's sister moved to her summer home in Spain, taking Christian's remaining son with her. They needed a clean slate in new surroundings, especially the teenage boy who had lost all of his immediate family in one month.

Sara took the photography job for the magazine and negotiated a deal where she could be based in England. She was required to travel to San Francisco once a month and she and George had already enjoyed three long weekends there.

George took the promotion and had the support of all of his peers.

"Are you ready, gorgeous?" George squeezed Sara's hand.

"Soo ready." She looked at him with her big shining eyes that were almost vibrating with excitement.

Together they pushed open the door of the estate agents' and went in to collect the keys to their brand-new home. They had opted for a new build. They were starting a life from scratch and leaving everything old in the past.

The estate agent greeted them with a dazzling smile and shook the keys at them. They handed over a bottle of wine and a thank-you card.

A week later, all of their new furniture had been delivered. They had dumped all their old furniture knowing that no one would buy it coming from the houses of horrors.

Sara had made a home in their new build. It was chic and Scandinavian-looking throughout with deep fluffy rugs, scatter cushions and ornamental candles. George wrapped his arms around her as they took it all in.

"You've done a stunning job. A real woman's touch. I love it."

Sara kissed him and opened her eyes. He was looking right at her.

"I love you so much, George Ramsay. I can't wait to be your wife."

He picked her up and carried her up the stairs. He stopped outside the bedroom door and looked at her lying in his arms.

"I can't wait, either. I need to make love to you right now." He gently laid her down on the bed and kicked the door closed with his foot as she pulled off his top and began to kiss his chest. He ran his hand through her hair and started kissing her neck. With each kiss her body would jolt beneath his.

"I've never loved anyone or anything like the way I love you, Sara. This is our time and I am never going to let you down or hurt you. Trust me."

She pulled his face to hers and kissed him passionately.

"We have a bed to christen, Mr Ramsay."

Later that day Sara was preparing the dining table for dinner with her parents. It was their first visit to the house and Sara was very excited about showing Ruth what she had learned from the dinner-party expert.

The house was not far from her parents' house. George said it would come in handy for when they decided to have babies. Sara wasn't against the idea but for now, she wanted to enjoy many more trips to America with the love of her life, just the two of them.

The doorbell rang and George welcomed his guests, taking their coats from them like the perfect host. Alan handed over a bottle of red. Ruth, too was armed with a gift. In its wrapping, it was large and square and looked as though it could be a painting.

Sara gave Ruth the grand tour. She made lots of ooh's and aah's at all the right times as doors and cupboards were opened.

"I tell you what love, you've done all right for yourself landing a place like this. It's very fancy. Much nicer than mine and your dad's first place."

"I know, Mum. I still have to pinch myself, really. It's been a hell of a six months."

"You can say that again."

Back downstairs, George had poured Alan an ale and they were talking sport while looking out of the kitchen window into the back garden. Ruth handed the gift to Sara.

"You can open it now, it's just a small gift for your new house."

"Oh, Mum, you didn't need to do anything. It's because of staying with you for months that we were able to put another ten grand down for the deposit."

"Don't talk about money dear, it's not ladylike."

Sara rolled her eyes and Ruth tutted. Sara peeled the wrapping paper off the large rectangular gift. It was a large photograph of George and Sara printed on canvas. He was pecking her on the cheek and she was smiling and holding a glass of champagne on Christmas Day.

"Oh, Mum. This is such a nice photo. I didn't even know it existed. I love it. Look, George. We look so happy."

"I took loads of pictures on Christmas Day and when I saw this one I knew I was going to get it blown up for you. I think you should put it in the dining room. The heart of the home." Sara gave her mother a hug and could feel her eyes welling up. "Don't cry darling," said Ruth. "It was meant to make you smile."

Sara laughed and reached for the tissues.

"I know. I just can't believe we are here. We survived and now look at us. We are so lucky."

George suggested they get some champagne out and have a toast. He retrieved a vintage bottle that he had bought earlier that day. A new house deserved a bottle of something special. He popped the cork and put it to Sara's mouth so as not to waste any of the overflow. She laughed as it went up her nose.

Alan tapped the top of his glass with a teaspoon.

"If it's OK with you, I'd like to do the toast. Sara... my baby girl. I can't believe we almost lost you and George, knowing you now, I can't imagine this family without you. You make my girl so happy and I know you will look after her. You can call me Dad and I will call you Son. I couldn't have asked for a better partner for her and now you have this house that you've achieved together. George, your promotion. Sara, your new job. You've got to look to the future now, kids, and try to put the past behind you. The world is your oyster. Sometimes, bad beginnings can lead to happy endings. Cheers."

Dear reader,

We hope you enjoyed reading *Trust Me*. Please take a moment to leave a review in Amazon, even if it's a short one. Your opinion is important to us.

Discover more books by Lucinda Lamont at https://www.nextchapter.pub/authors/lucinda-lamont-contemporary-fiction-author

Want to know when one of our books is free or discounted for Kindle? Join the newsletter at http://eepurl.com/bqqB3H

Best regards,

Lucinda Lamont and the Next Chapter Team

You might also like:
Layla's Score by Andy Rausch

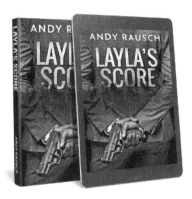

To read the first chapter for free, head to:
https://www.nextchapter.pub/books/laylas-score

ACKNOWLEDGMENTS

I would like to thank Donna Maria McCarthy. Your support for me is endless and you always make me smile. Let's never stop getting the telescope out to review books!

To Michael Collins. Thank you for sharing some of your Scotland Yard memories with me. I hope I have written this in an accurate style. To anyone reading this, Mick makes the best handmade chocolate on the South Coast. (Choccablock ltd)

Printed in Great Britain
by Amazon